THE EASTER
BUNNY INVASION!

Written, designed and published by Clifford James Hayes

www.hayesdesign.co.uk

The Easter Bunny Invasion!, 2018 edition.

THE EASTER
BUNNY INVASION!

CLIFFORD JAMES HAYES

www.hayesdesign.co.uk

BOOKS AVAILABLE:

Augustus, the Hairy Zummabeest
The Slug that Saved Christmas
The Easter Bunny Invasion
The Easter Bunny's Outer Space Adventure
The Easter Bunny's Undersea Adventure
The Ugly Mermaid (illustrated)
Grandma Grunt
Horrid Horatia
Hairy Tales
(A Collection of Stories for Naughty Boys and Girls)
Verity Fruitt and My Magic Gonk

For other titles available (printed and ebook formats),
do a search for 'Clifford James Hayes' on Amazon.

CUSTOMARY AUTHOR'S NOTE:

It may seem as if there are many, many shocking inaccuracies and punctuation niggles lurking within this book's waffle – however, these are entirely deliberate. Please bear in mind that my tales are set in the land of Hairy Make-Believe, where bad grammar is commonplace and quite the norm.

Well, that's my excuse – and I'm sticking to it.

CHAPTER ONE

THE EASTER BUNNY,
AND HER LITTLE BUNNY HELPERS

You probably know all about Christmas - how each and every year, Santa's elves spend months and months of their time making millions and millions of toys - just so that the big old guy in the red suit can fly round the world with his reindeer and hand out presents to all the children of the world. Well, hand them out to the GOOD ones, that is; if you've been naughty, he certainly WON'T be paying you a visit!

But did you know that something similar happens at Easter? That someone out there has to make all the millions and millions of delicious chocolate eggs that

children receive, and that someone then has to deliver them all? I'm not talking about Santa and his elves here - they're all usually fast asleep during the spring, catching up on some much needed rest and relaxation, before they get down to the task of making next Christmas's toys and gifts. No, when it comes to handing out gifts at Easter time, we're talking about someone else entirely.

I am, of course, referring to the Easter Bunny. I'm sure you've heard of him too. Or should I say, HER - because the Easter Bunny happens to be a LADY Bunny, not a Mister Bunny, which is a common mistake most people make. She's got a proper name, too - she's not just known as 'the Easter Bunny' - that would just be silly. It's a fairly humdrum name she's got - Mildred - but it's a name, nonetheless. Not a lot of people know she's called Mildred, but it's true.

And just like Santa, Mildred the Easter Bunny needs more than a little help and assistance, when it comes to making and delivering all those deliciously scrumptious chocolate eggs. It never used to be the case; she used to be able to do everything herself. But what with there being far too many people in the world these days, and global warming, and all that other unpleasant stuff you see on the TV news, it eventually made sense for the Easter Bunny to get some helpers, to help make her job a little easier.

Mildred's helpers also happen to be bunnies - but whereas the Easter Bunny is six feet tall and weighs 252 pounds, her helper bunnies are all normal sized; though they're certainly not *normal-brained*. You see, helper bunnies are all pretty smart indeed - well, they'd have to be, otherwise they'd be no use to her at all, and just sit around all day - nibbling at things, making the occasional 'squeak', hopping occasionally and dropping little brown poo pellets everywhere.

"Where do these smarter, helper bunnies come from?" you may ask. Good question. The answer is a strange one; they come from the same place as normal bunnies, because that's exactly what they used to be.

It was the Easter Bunny who made them clever. Every year, she would gather together as many ordinary bunnies as she needed (from country fields and such places), then 'fzapp' them with a device she had invented, called the 'brain-ray'. This would make them incredibly smart, and make them perfect helpers when it came to making her delicious chocolate Easter eggs.

Every helper bunny was given an important mission. First, they had to collect the cocoa, sugar, milk and other ingredients needed for the chocolate, from all the best plantations and farms the world had to offer. Then they had to help in the making of the chocolate, at the Easter Bunny's chocolate egg factory (which was enormously huge, and shaped liked a giant egg - you'd love it!). Once the chocolate eggs were all made, the helpers assisted with the wrapping and packaging of the eggs - first wrapping them in colourful tin foil, and then placing them all into boxes, for dispatching to the world's children. And it was the dispatching that the bunnies love best! For once all the chocolate eggs were ready, the helper bunnies all got to deliver the eggs themselves.

Yes, gone were the days when the Easter Bunny used to deliver all the eggs alone - with so many children in the world, the egg delivery system just had to be modernised. At the top of the chocolate egg factory is a tiny room, containing an aircraft pilot's chair, a wall of important-looking switches and buttons, and an egg-shaped steering wheel.

When the Easter Bunny sits down in the chair, she is ready to deliver the eggs - as the giant, egg-shaped factory also happens to be a giant, egg-shaped flying machine! So each and every year, just before Easter, the Easter Bunny pushed a few buttons and pulled a few levers, and the egg-shaped building would detach itself from the ground and lift off into the sky on its delivery mission.

Once the flying factory is airborne, the helper

bunnies all make their way to the 'dispatch bay' - this is a giant room at the bottom of the building, where all the millions of chocolate eggs are stored. The helper bunnies each put on a pair of goggles and a parachute, and grab a chocolate egg box. Then, as the first town or village comes into view, the Easter Bunny pulls another lever - and a pair of doors swing open down in the dispatch bay.

You may be able to guess what happens next; once the giant flying machine is hovering over a town, some of the helper bunnies launch themselves out of the open doors! When they are safely away from the flying factory ship, they pull their parachute cords and gently fly down on to the roofs of the building below. After they've landed, they make their way down the buildings' chimneys and deliver the chocolate eggs (as you may have guessed, they got the whole 'jumping down the chimney' idea from Santa and the elves).

Now, once all this is done, you might think the helper bunnies would have to somehow make their way back to the flying machine. But this isn't so - for, after the eggs have been safely delivered, something strange and slightly magical happens; the helper bunnies become 'normal' bunnies again. They lose their cleverness and their chocolate egg-making skills, not to mention their daring parachuting abilities. After they have all completed their mission, they just become simple, slightly brainless, hoppity-floppity rabbits once more, and nibble and hop and flollop about in fields and gardens; which is PRECISELY why you suddenly see so many bunnies hopping about at that time of year!

Actually, the reason why the helper bunnies became normal bunnies again wasn't really down to anything mysterious or magical - it was simply down to the fact that Mildred the Easter Bunny fzapped them with her brain-ray back into normal bunnies again, once Easter had passed, as she thought it was kinder that they should return to the way nature had intended them to be.

The Easter Bunny had never been sure why there always seemed to be quite so many rabbits - she'd turn her back on one for just a moment, and when she looked again, FOUR MORE bunnies had suddenly arrived out of nowhere! They certainly were mysterious little things, and she had often suspected that if you got them wet they would multiply like crazy - just like the furry little critters she'd seen in a movie one time. Yes, the Easter Bunny had to be careful she didn't get TOO MANY of the floppy-eared things - otherwise there would be absolute pandemonium! But as every coming year meant a new batch of Easter eggs needed to be

made, she had no choice but to 'fzapp' bunnies into new helpers, so that the egg-making process could start all over again.

To be honest, I think all the years of egg-making had turned the Easter Bunny a bit bonkers. Just look at the facts, if you don't believe me; she was a six foot tall bunny rabbit (called Mildred), who spent year after year after year making millions of chocolate eggs for all the children of the world. In order for her to do this, she regularly 'fzapped' innocent little rabbits with her brain-ray invention, in order to turn them into hardworking, intelligent ones. (And I haven't mentioned yet that she had built rows and rows of little cottages for them all to live in, while they spent their egg-making time with her). Then, after Easter had passed, she would fzapp them all once more, in order to turn them back into mindless little carrot-munchers. On the few spare days she had each year, she spent all her time waterskiing, took the occasional holiday in the North Pole (to chill out with Santa and the elves) and had invented a gigantic, egg-shaped, egg-making factory, that could also turn into an aircraft! Impressive; yes. Barking mad; definitely.

But whether she was a bit loopy in the head or otherwise, no-one could deny that it was very hard work being the Easter Bunny, and that she oozed kindness and generosity. And Mildred never complained; her life was all about making Easter eggs, and dispatching Easter eggs. And that was the way it had been for many, many, many years now. Until quite recently, in fact - when something - or rather, someone - decided to stir things up a little ...

The particular year I'm referring to started out like any other. Winter passed, and springtime came. Daffodils and bluebells were soon poking their heads through the last of the winter snow, new-born lambs were frolicking alongside their mothers in the farmers' pastures, and people everywhere were beginning the task of making repairs and renovations, after long months of wintry weather had taken its toll on their homes.

As it was springtime, Santa Claus and his helper elves were all fast asleep by now - taking a well-earned rest after months of labour in the toy factory. Which meant that - like every other year - it was time for the Easter Bunny and her little helpers to bounce into action and get the chocolate egg-making underway.

The Easter Bunny was already doing a great job this particular year. As always, she had fzapped a few thousand bunnies with her brain-ray to make them clever, then sent them all on a mission as soon as they had gotten used to being super-smart and helpful. These brave and courageous little bunnies had to travel to the four corners of the globe, to seek out and gather together the finest ingredients for all the chocolate eggs. And within weeks they had all safely returned, which was something of a blessing as they faced many perils on their journeys.

Each and every one of her helpers had been decked out in cool 'adventure' gear for their journeys - they had night-vision goggles and wireless headsets, and bush knives for cutting through dense undergrowth. They wore camouflage-patterned outfits, and carried backpacks full of the type of survival equipment bunnies might need in the wildernesses of the world.

From Columbia they had fetched back the very, very best cocoa beans they could find - beans that had to be grown on plants that are exactly 3,037 feet above sea level, so that they make the chocolate taste utterly splendiferous. From the beautiful island of Mauritius they had purchased the finest sugar cane the world has to offer - sugar cane so absolutely sweet and delicious that the locals are forbidden to eat it themselves, as once they begin to munch on the stuff they find they just can't stop (this is why my father-in-law lost all his teeth by the age of thirty, but that's another story).

And, last but not least, some of the bunnies had bought back the smoothest-tasting vanilla essence in the world - which I'm sure you all know can ONLY be purchased from the island of Oom-Balla-Papa-Lalla-Shaka-Manaloko.

Once she had gathered together the *mountains* of ingredients needed for the millions of chocolate eggs, the Easter Bunny set to work in the egg factory's kitchen. There, she oversaw the cooking of all the deliciously gooey liquid chocolate. Hundreds of bunny-rabbit helpers (in little chef hats) busied themselves as they followed Mildred the Easter Bunny's instructions; they were all determined to make this year's chocolate eggs even scrummier than the eggs from the year before - which wouldn't be too easy, as last year's eggs had been of exceptionally good quality.

Finally, satisfied that her helpers had come up with some absolutely heavenly-tasting chocolate goo, the Easter Bunny gave instruction for the liquid chocolate to be sent over to the *egg-shaping production line*.

The egg-shaping production line was where the helper bunnies turned the runny, gooey chocolate into solid, egg-shaped Easter eggs. There was always a great deal of squirty, squelchy, bubbling noises from the factory's pumps and tubes and pipes as thousands of gallons of hot, runny chocolate arrived from the kitchen. The helper bunnies then used squirting machines to plop out the runny chocolate into thousands of egg-shaped containers - which were then cooled a little, to make the chocolate go hard.

And so, in what really was next to no time at all, the factory soon had an ENORMOUS pyramid of brand new Easter eggs, that reached almost to the factory's ceiling!

Now, you might expect me to say that the helper bunnies then set about wrapping the eggs in coloured foil, before packing them into boxes. And that once this had all been done, the Easter Bunny sat herself down in her pilot's seat, launched the factory into the air, and flew the bunnies and eggs across the world - so that they could then be delivered to millions of children all keen to tuck into a scrumptious chocolate egg. And indeed, were it any other year, this is EXACTLY what would have happened. But on *this* particular year, a very different turn of events made Easter quite unlike ANYTHING that had come before - as we shall soon see ...

The Easter Bunny was exceptionally proud of all her workers this particular year; they really had managed to make the finest-tasting chocolate she had ever tasted, and they had all worked their little paws to

the bone with all their efforts. And so she decided to REWARD her thousands of furry, long-eared helpers.

It was late on Thursday afternoon when she assembled them all in the main factory, in order to make an announcement.

"Dear friends," she began, "I am so TRULY delighted with all you have achieved so far this year. You bravely searched through the thickest jungles and over the harshest terrains to find me the very best of ingredients, and have delivered the most delicious chocolate as a result." She looked admiringly at the mountain of chocolate eggs they had all produced. "As you can see, we are well ahead of schedule, in regards to making this year's eggs - and once more, this is all down to your efforts; yours and yours alone. And so - as we're all doing so well this year - I think it only fair that you dudes have yourselves a break and take the next few days off!"

There were gasps and cheers from the bunnies as they took in what the Easter Bunny had said; this had never happened before, in living memory. Usually at this time of year the bunnies were furiously trying to keep up with their schedule - so it seemed like a small Eastery miracle that for once they were actually well ahead in terms of what needed to be done.

"Off you go, then!" the Easter Bunny called out.

"I'll see you all on Monday morning, at 9 o'clock sharp. Then we can crack-on with the tin foil wrapping and the ribbon-tying, and get the eggs dispatched for another year!"

The bunnies didn't need telling twice; they gleefully wriggled out of their work clothes and hopped and jumped out of the factory's main entrance, setting off back to the rows and rows of lovely miniature cottages the Easter Bunny had provided for them all to live in. Glad to see such happiness on her hardworking helpers' little faces, the Easter Bunny joyfully followed them out.

CHAPTER TWO

SOMEBODY'S STOLEN OUR
EGG FACTORY!

The Easter Bunny decided she would spend her long weekend waterskiing (which was the Easter Bunny's favourite hobby, as I may have mentioned). She locked the factory doors behind her, after making sure everyone had left - leaving the egg factory completely empty.

Empty, that is, except for one rather crafty individual - who slyly slinked out of the shadows from behind some of the egg factory's pipes and machinery, when all had gone quiet. This crafty individual had always admired the Easter Bunny's impressive flying machine egg factory, and had often wondered how he might one day get his sly and devious paws on it. He often crept about like this, sneaking in and out of the factory when it suited, thanks to knowing where some of the factory's pipes opened up in the surrounding countryside.

Once inside, he'd slip from room to room, discovering all the Easter Bunny's plans and secrets. Getting in and out of the factory wasn't a problem for a sly and crafty individual like him.

He liked to listen-in on the Easter Bunny's conversations, and find out what kind of chocolate eggs she would be making each year. Not that he liked her eggs - he absolutely hated chocolate - but he did like to be sly and nosey (just for the sake of it), as you never know when knowing things might come in very useful.

But the final reason he liked to come into the factory was certainly by far the worst - because one thing he liked to do more than anything else in the world was to catch and EAT the helper bunnies! He'd slink around in the shadows, waiting for one of the little rabbits to be alone, then - pounce! - he'd quickly jump out from the dark and grab the poor, unsuspecting little bunny. And, due to their being *so many* of the unfortunate little creatures, no-one had ever noticed when a bunny suddenly disappeared, and no-one ever knew what unpleasantness went on in the quieter, darker corners of the factory.

This sly, crafty and frankly horrible individual did of course have a name - one that summed him up quite nicely. For he was Foxington 'Foxy' McFox - the foxiest fox in all of Foxtown!

Everyone knew his dastardly reputation; Foxy McFox and his sly and nasty foxy mates from Foxtown had been seen prowling around in the surrounding fields on many an occasion. But no-one knew he'd actually managed to find a way INTO the factory, nor that he'd been slinking around inside the building for a very long time indeed.

With the building now empty, the sly old fox quietly made his way down a flight of stairs so he could stand on the factory's ground floor. He looked up at the giant pyramid of chocolate Easter eggs, to admire it.

"That's a lot of chocolate," he murmured to himself. He looked around the immense factory, impressed; this factory had everything, and looked so much bigger now that it was missing its thousands of bunny workers. There were automated production lines, conveyor belts, hydraulic lifts, stacking trucks, packaging machinery - you name it, it had it.

"It's got EVERYTHING I need," he slyly cackled to himself, as his schemes and plans turned

over in his head. He turned again to look up at the mountain of eggs that dwarfed him. "And with the Easter Bunny out the way, the timing is perfect. But first I need to get rid of all this horrible chocolate."

Finding the factory's entrance doors locked, Foxy McFox made his way back through the labyrinth of tubes and pipes he'd so often used to get in and out of the building. Within minutes he was back outside, and set off toward the helper bunnies' cottages.

Little Fluffikins and Denzil were two ordinary, respectable and very well-to-do helper bunnies. Denzil wore smart waistcoats and horn-rimmed spectacles, while Little Fluffikins liked to model her appearance on the famous film idols from days gone by. Unfortunately for Little Fluffikins and Denzil, they lived in the cottage that lay closest to the pipe entrance Foxy McFox secretly used to enter the factory - which meant the door to their cottage was the one he came knocking at, in order to carry out his wicked scheme.

Denzil answered the knock at the door, and was understandably dismayed when he was grabbed by the ears and roughly thrown into a smelly old sack. Moments later, the same thing happened to Little Fluffikins.

The nasty old fox carried them back inside the

factory - through tunnel after tunnel they were painfully dragged, up and down and along twisting pipes and underfloor ducts until they reached a shadowy hole in a side wall. The fox carried them both through this, then dragged them a little further - before removing them from the sack and once more lifting them up by the ears. They naturally protested and complained about this dreadfully rough handling, but were amazed to suddenly find themselves in the middle of the egg factory's production room. The familiar conveyor belts and factory machinery stood all around them, and the giant pyramid of chocolate eggs towered nearby.

"What are your names?" asked Foxy McFox.

"Little Fluffikins," said Little Fluffikins, scowling defiantly at her captor.

"D-Denzil," answered Denzil, more timidly.

"I'm delighted to meet you both," said Foxy, as he finally put them down on the ground.

"Y-you're not going to eat us, are you?" asked Denzil, who obviously was hoping for a 'no', but was also wishing he hadn't asked the question in the first place.

"Of course not!" chuckled Foxy, with a grin. "You're far more useful to me alive."

"What do you mean?" asked Little Fluffikins, who

wasn't as nervous as Denzil, and who certainly wasn't afraid of this horrid old fox - whether he intended to eat them, or otherwise.

Foxy McFox lowered his long nose to her own little button nose, until they almost touched. "I mean, Young Miss, that all I want of you and young Denzil here is to do what you little bunnies always do - just be yourselves."

"You're not making any sense at all," snorted Little Fluffikins dismissively.

"Well, perhaps not," sighed the fox, as he curled his bushy red tail around her, "but that doesn't really matter. I've seen you little critters out there in the countryside - hopping around, eating anything and everything, and multiplying like - well, like rabbits. All I need of you is for you to eat this here little mountain of chocolate eggs for me."

Little Fluffikins laughed at the fox, making him scowl. "I think you've got the wrong kind of bunnies," she mocked. "We're 'helper' bunnies, not those completely brainless, wild little things that jump around in fields all day, eating everything they see. We're NOTHING like those simple creatures."

Little Fluffikins' retorts gave Denzil a little confidence. "Yes, and I find it highly unlikely we'd be inclined to eat this mountain of eggs, even if we could,

and even if we wanted to. We HAVE just spent several months of our lives making those things, you know."

Foxy McFox sighed. "I understand all that," he answered. "I really do. You two are smart; I can see that. But 'smartness' isn't something I need right now."

"Well then, in that case you've obviously got the wrong bunnies and you can let us go," replied Little Fluffikins, her furry little arms crossed in frustration. "Sort of now-ish."

"Oh, I still need you," answered the fox. "But not your smartness, like I say. And this is where THIS comes in handy." Foxy McFox pulled something out of his tweed jacket's inside pocket. It was silver-metallic, with colourful wires poking out of the sides - it looked like some kind of ray-gun.

"W-what's that?" asked Denzil, warily. "And what do you intend to do with it?"

"Oh, nothing more than what your glorious leader, the Easter Bunny, was going to do with it," replied the fox, as he tapped it against his left paw. "You see, I came across this ingenious item during one of my regular 'investigations' into this facility. Normally it is attached to the side of the egg factory, and is powered by the building's electric supply - but with a bit of tinkering I've been able to make it run off a battery cell." Foxy McFox handled the device, looking at it carefully.

"Denzil asked you what it does," said Little Fluffikins, impatiently. "I'd like to know, too."

"Shall I show you?" said the fox, who then pointed and fired it at Denzil. With a flash of green light and a 'fzapp!' noise, Denzil was immediately transformed from a well-dressed, intelligent-looking helper bunny into an ordinary, docile wild rabbit. The bunny scratched at his ears with one of his hind paws, and uttered a few squeaks. Little Fluffikins looked at the bunny that had been Denzil in horror.

With a slimy grin, the fox continued to speak - seeing as stroppy-madam Little Fluffikins appeared to be lost for words for once. "I'd always wondered how the Easter Bunny turned you lot into smart rabbits, and then back into dumb ones, once she'd gotten you to do all the egg-making work for her." He chuckled at the aghast look on the lady bunny's face. "And now I know. It's all down to this little ray-gun."

"That's beastly!" replied Little Fluffikins, eventually. "And I can't believe the Easter Bunny would do such a thing to us; turning us back into mindless eating machines."

Foxy McFox shrugged. "Oh, I can understand it, really," he replied. "I'd probably do the same. There's just SO MANY of yer. It's the only way she can keep your numbers down - unless she eats you all." He smiled cruelly, as his plans and schemes popped up in his mind once more. "But I've got a much better way of keeping you all under control; just you wait and see."

Little Fluffikins backed away slightly from the fox, as he pointed the ray-gun toward her. "You keep that dreadful thing away from me," she warned.

"Sorry, love," he replied, "I like you; I really do. You're smart. But like I said; smartness isn't something I need off you right now." The ray-gun fired again, and Little Fluffikins was fzapped into just another mindless, fluffy bunny rabbit.

With Little Fluffikins and Denzil hopping around contentedly in front of him, Foxy McFox put away the ray-gun and rubbed his paws together. "Right, now ... let's see. Two bunnies; one mountain of eggs. How long will it take them to eat them all?" He looked down at his watch, to check the time. He looked up again, to discover the two bunnies had suddenly turned into five.

"How DO they do that?" he said to himself, shaking his head in disbelief. "Oh well," he shrugged, "I'll come back in the morning, and see how they've all got on."

As promised, Foxy McFox came back in the morning, to see how they'd all got on.

He was very impressed; the millions of eggs had all been eaten, and *thousands* of mindless little bunnies were now hopping about the factory floor. They were everywhere, in fact - sitting in the machinery, hopping about on the pipes that criss-crossed the ceiling high above, riding on the conveyor belts as they trundled round and round - absolutely everywhere. And of course, as they'd eaten a mountain of chocolate, there were plenty of unpleasant little rabbit droppings all over the place. Foxy McFox couldn't be more pleased.

"Aha! - Stage One of my plan is complete," he laughed aloud. "And now it's time for Stage Two."

While all the chaos in the factory was beginning to unravel, Mildred the Easter Bunny was having the best of times. She'd promised herself a weekend of waterskiing, and that's exactly what she was doing - whizzing up and down the lake that ran alongside the helper bunnies' rows of cottages. Similarly, all the helper bunnies were also appreciating their unexpected time off, and either lazed about in their cottages or went for leisurely hops along the lakeside.

It was the bunnies taking leisurely hops along the lakeside who first realised something was wrong. They heard the boom of rocket engines being ignited, and looked over in the direction of the factory. The bunnies looked on in confusion and dismay as they realised the egg factory was lifting off into the sky. It made a pulsating 'wubba-wubba-wubba-wubba' sound as it rose ever higher. Frantically, they waved and hollered at the Easter Bunny, but she was so absorbed in her waterskiing that she completely failed to notice the launch of her flying factory.

Until it was too late, that is. When she finally spotted the egg ship taking off she lost her balance on her skis, and flolloped face-down into the lake's water with a mighty splash. It was a soaking wet, horrified-looking Easter Bunny that eventually scrambled on to the muddy banks of the lake.

Many helper bunnies went to assist her, as she slipped and slid in the squodgy mud. As soon as she was on firmer land, the Easter Bunny trotted over to the factory grounds as fast as her big, padded feet would take her, with many of her helpers hopping along close behind. The other rabbits were quickly raised from their rests in the cottages, until all were assembled together in the factory grounds.

There was little to see, of course; where once the egg factory had stood, there was now only a huge, empty space.

"Stolen!" exclaimed the Easter Bunny out loud. "Stolen from under our very noses!"

"But who would DO such a thing?" asked an elderly lady bunny, who went by the name of Mrs Fluffywinkle. "And why?"

"There's only one I know of who could do such a dastardly thing," said a well-built (but somewhat timid) bunny named Marmaduke. He looked off into the distance, and saw that the egg factory was heading east as it approached the horizon. "Over yonder lies Foxtown; that's where the egg factory is headed. And we all know who lives there."

"Sly old Foxy McFox!" exclaimed everyone together. "And all the other foxes!"

"You're right," agreed the still dripping-wet Easter Bunny. "And now it's up to us all to put a stop to whatever scheme that foul, sneaky, slinky fox is up to!" And without another word, she began trotting eastwards, with her army of helper bunnies hopping and jumping close behind.

Unfortunately, they were all making something of a wasted journey. By the time they reached Foxtown, there wasn't a single fox to be seen. Gone too was the flying egg factory.

"He must have stopped to pick up all the other foxes," said Marmaduke. "But what on Earth is he up to?"

"Oh, something sly and devious and cruel, I've no

doubt," replied the Easter Bunny, with a scowl. "Taking all the other foxes means he can't do it on his own - so whatever he's up to, I'd say it must be something big."

It WAS something big. Something VERY big, actually, and very bad. As the bunnies had guessed, Foxy McFox had indeed stopped at Foxtown to pick up all his foxy friends; he would certainly need them, for what he had in store.

He piloted the egg factory himself. He'd known all about the Easter Bunny's pilot chair, and her room full of buttons and switches and levers that were used to make the factory fly. Foxy flew the ship with ease; during his many secret visits to the factory he'd spent lots of time working out what all the buttons and switches and levers did, and had no trouble landing the ship again, when he'd arrived at Foxtown to pick up all his foxy friends.

If anyone had been watching, they'd have seen the foxes load dozens of unmarked crates on to the egg ship - crates full of things Foxy needed for this schemes and plans to work.

Once all was done, Foxy McFox then took off once more. The egg ship made its distinctive 'wubba-wubba-wubba-wubba' sound as it lifted skyward, then headed to the first of the destinations he planned to fly to. Foxy's plan was underway.

CHAPTER THREE

THE EASTER BUNNY INVASION!

There was a castle in a nearby town. This was owned by an enormous (and exceptionally unpleasant) lady slug, called Horatia Vulgaria Grymgusset. Most people tended to call her *Horrid Horatia*, because of all the selfish, horrible things she did to other people.

Foxy McFox didn't like Horatia the lady slug one little bit. He didn't care about the fact that she was horrid to everyone else, but he certainly did care about the fact she had once been horrid to him; they were sworn enemies, as far as he was concerned.

You see, Horatia had once shot Foxy up the

backside with her blunderbuss shotgun, when he had been slinking around her castle's grounds. As you can imagine, the pain of this and the discomfort of the pellets that were stuck in his bottom as a result of the shotgun blast gave Foxy some very bad memories of his encounter with Horatia. So now, as far as Foxy was concerned, it was time for him to get his own back on her.

He flew the egg ship directly over her castle. Below, Foxy could see the many shiny, polished hovercrafts that belonged to Horatia the lady slug. She was very precious about her hovercrafts, and could get very nasty indeed if anyone dared to touch their shiny bonnets and sides.

There were two reasons why she had so many hovercrafts. First, having so many hovercrafts made her feel rich and important. Second, having so many hovercrafts was an effective way of stopping other people from parking their own vehicles anywhere near the castle. That's how selfish (and rather silly) Horatia was, you see.

Foxy McFox's foxy friends were all working in the dispatch bay, and were knee-deep in bunnies (and up to their ankles in rabbit droppings). The foxes couldn't believe it; every time they blinked or looked away, it seemed as though there were twice as many rabbits as there had been just moments before. But they certainly weren't complaining; they had plenty of fresh food hopping about in front of them, and realised they were on to a good thing here. But they also had a job to do, and were busy doing it. One or two of the foxes were unpacking the contents of the crates they had fetched with them, while some of the other foxes were taking the contents and getting them ready for later.

"How's it looking down there?" called Foxy to the others, via the microphone. "Are we ready to offload a few rabbits yet?"

"No problem at all, boss," replied Clodwell, a weaselly-sounding fox. "You could offload half a million of them, and you wouldn't even notice the difference. It's wall-to-wall rabbits down here. And we've shovelled a load of them down to the dispatch bay for ya, just like you asked."

"Bombs away, then!" replied Foxy McFox, and he pulled the lever that opened the dispatch bay doors. They swung wide open, and - with a fading 'wheeeeeeeee' sound - thousands of bunnies suddenly dropped from the sky and on to the castle and shiny hovercrafts below.

Horatia the lady slug had been contentedly wallowing in a vat of slime when she heard what sounded like very heavy rain coming down. Grumbling

and cursing, she immediately got out of her vat and slithered to her castle's front door; she hadn't expected wet weather, and now she'd have to very speedily get her many open-topped hovercrafts safely under cover.

Horatia opened the huge front door to her castle, and prepared herself to slither in the rain toward the first of her precious vehicles. Instead, she was horrified to discover it had rained rabbits. Thousands of them. They hopped about on top of her shiny hovercrafts, leaving little brown pellets of poo all over the shiny, waxy paintwork. They sat lazily on the ramparts of her castle, and munched contentedly on her prize garden patch of lettuces and cabbages.

"I need my blunderbuss!" she bellowed, and hastily slithered back inside to find her shotgun. She was back moments later, firing her gun wildly in all directions. Luckily for the bunnies, her rage had made her a pretty lousy shot that day - she made plenty of bullet holes in her beloved hovercrafts, but none whatsoever in any of the rabbits.

"That'll teach her," Foxy McFox cackled as he watched everything from the skies above. "We'll come back in a week, boys," he called out to the other foxes. "Her castle will be full to the brim with rabbits by then! She'll pay us a FORTUNE to get rid of all the bunnies for her, after a week of all that madness."

Now, you might say to yourself 'What's so bad about some bunny rabbits hopping around everywhere?' And normally, you'd be right. But we're not talking about 'some' bunnies, here - we're talking about a swarm. A plague! A tidal wave!! And if nothing else, the sheer noise of them all hopping around would be enough to drive most people insane ... *Bounce. Bounce. Flippity hop. Squeak! Shuffle-shuffle. Sproink! Boink! Shuffle-shuffle. Bounce, bounce, bounce, bounce. Squeak! Nibble nibble. Boing! Squeak! Sproing! Bounce. Bounce. Flippity hop. Squeak! Shuffle-shuffle. Sproink! Boink! Shuffle-shuffle. Bounce, bounce, bounce, bounce. Squeak! Nibble nibble. Boing! Squeak! Sproing! Bounce. Bounce. Flippity hop. Squeak! Shuffle-shuffle. Sproink! Boink! Shuffle-shuffle. Bounce, bounce, bounce, bounce. Squeak! Nibble nibble. Boing! Squeak! Sproing! Bounce. Bounce. Flippity hop. Squeak! Shuffle-shuffle. Sproink! Boink! Shuffle-shuffle. Bounce, bounce, bounce, bounce. Squeak! Nibble nibble. Boing! Squeak! Sproing! Bounce. Bounce. Flippity hop. Squeak! Shuffle-shuffle. Sproink! Boink! Shuffle-shuffle. Bounce, bounce, bounce, bounce. Squeak! Nibble nibble. Boing! Squeak! Sproing! Flippity hop.*

That was Foxy's plan, you see - he was going to terrorise ANYONE and EVERYONE with his seemingly endless supply of bunny rabbits. And it was

going to make him very rich indeed. Or at least, that was the FIRST part of his plan. The second part was absolutely dreadful, but we'll get to that in time.

Foxy threw a handful of business cards out of the pilot's window, so that Horatia would know who to call when she was ready to have the rabbits removed. The cards said 'Bunny Exterminators' in big letters, with a phone number and email address underneath.

"Where to next, boss?" asked Clodwell.

"Aw, you'll see, soon enough," replied Foxy with a cackle. "An' I don't want to spoil all the fun. Just put yer jacket's on, lads; it's gonna get pretty cold soon."

The egg ship flew due north, to the North Pole. All was quiet there; the chill winds howled across the icy landscape, but there was no-one to be seen in Elf Town or the surrounding area. As mentioned earlier, because it was springtime Santa and his elves would be fast asleep, catching up on some well-deserved rest after all their hard work getting the world's Christmas presents ready.

Not everyone was asleep, however, as Foxy discovered when he arrived at the North Pole's landing strip. The wily old fox gently landed the egg ship on to the snow-lashed tarmac of the airport runway, its 'wubba-wubba-wubba-wubba' engine noise slowing to a halt as it touched-down.

He looked out of the pilot's viewing windows. In the distance, Foxy could see Santa's Elf Factory, along with all the surrounding houses and cottages where the elves lived.

Shortly, the old fox noticed that a large, greeny-brown creature (wearing a Santa hat) was slithering from the Elf Factory to see who this new arrival was. Foxy peered down at him - it was another giant slug! And riding on his back was one of the little elves!

"Two slugs in one day, eh?" mused Foxy. It was a funny coincidence indeed - but really, it was just one of those things. You see, in case you didn't know it, the North Pole these days has its own giant slug, called Clarence. But whereas Horatia the slug was foul and horrible, Clarence was very helpful - pretty brainless, I'll admit - but still very helpful. If you've read about his adventures, you'll know that Clarence the slug saved the day one Christmas, when Santa had gone a bit bonkers and had been unable to deliver all the presents. Clarence the slug was very well-respected, as a result. You may also know that the North Pole's Elf Doctor had fallen in love with Clarence, and taken to riding on Clarence's back at all times. And it was the Elf Doctor who now spoke, calling loudly up to the pilot's window.

"Ahoy, Easter Bunny!" he shouted. "What brings you to these parts at this time of year? Everyone's still hibernating, after the Christmas rush!"

The Elf Doctor, as you may have guessed, assumed it was the Easter Bunny who had fetched the egg ship up to the North Pole. The Elf Doctor knew the Easter Bunny quite well, as she had often visited Santa in the past, in early summer - which is a time of year when they both had little to do. So you may not be too surprised to hear that seeing Foxy McFox stick his long foxy nose out of the pilot's window was NOT something the Elf Doctor was quite expecting.

"Do I LOOK like the Easter Bunny?" remarked Foxy McFox, in snidey response.

"No, you most certainly do not," was the firm reply. "But I know who YOU are; you're that Foxy McFox - the Easter Bunny's mentioned you in the past. And you're a beastly cad and a bounder, from what I've heard."

"Aw, that's not a very nice way to welcome visitors," replied the fox. "Especially one bearing gifts."

"Gifts?" said the Elf Doctor, very warily. "What sort of gifts? And who for?"

"Nice gifts," replied the fox, with a smile. "FLUFFY gifts. Fluffy gifts for everyone. Even got one for your pet slug."

"He's not a pet!" barked the Elf Doctor, angrily. "He's called Clarence. And I love him very much."

"Oh, well … whatever floats your boat," answered Foxy, rolling his eyes, and sighing. He was getting a little impatient. "Look; do you want these presents, or not? I'm leaving them here anyway, regardless."

The Elf Doctor looked around; there was no-one else to help him decide what to do. Santa usually took care of everything when it came to decisions, he explained to the fox, but Santa was fast asleep - and he wouldn't appreciate being woken up for the sake of some gifts a sneaky old fox was leaving for him.

Foxy McFox shrugged in an 'it's not really my problem, is it?' kind of way.

"Oh, all right," said the elf, eventually. "Just leave them here, on the runway, and Clarence and I will take them back to Elf Town."

"That was the plan," replied the fox with a cackle, and he pulled on the lever that swung open the dispatch-bay doors. Seconds later, thousands upon thousands of fluffy bunnies fell out of the open doors, and on to the runway tarmac.

"Agh!" screeched the Elf Doctor, like a terrified little girl. "Bunnies!"

Clarence the slug reared up in shock, and made a surprised 'mooing' noise as the army of rabbits swarmed about him and hopped all over his slimy body.

"Happy Easter!" chuckled Foxy, as he watched them bounce and hop and spring and jump and flollop towards Elf Town.

"You absolute fiend!" shouted the Elf Doctor. "They'll eat EVERYTHING! All the food, all the toys, all the town - everything!"

"Heh-heh-heh - that's right," sneered the fox, as he threw another bundle of his business cards out of the window. "They WILL eat everything - I guarantee it. And that'll serve you right for being so goodie-goodie every Christmas, handing out presents to all those horrible little kiddies. They don't deserve anything - except a good kick up the backside - as far as I'm concerned. But I'll be back in a week, and then we can discuss terms in regards to me getting rid of them for you. It's probably best you wake Santa up now. Toodle pip!" And with that, Foxy McFox launched the egg ship into the sky once more.

This terrible pattern of events continued for seven more days. Foxy McFox flew from one destination to the next, unleashing his seemingly never-ending supply of fluffy bunnies. Nobody knew where he would strike next. It truly was a worldwide bunny invasion!

After Elf Town, he flew the flying factory ship to

another destination in the North Pole - the Walrus Queendom of Lady Karacas. This icy realm had long been the domain all the walruses. Many other sea creatures (including the orcas, the polar bears and Binky the Squid) often came there also, to pay tribute to its majestic Queen. But now it too fell foul of the bunny invasion, as Foxy McFox offloaded another half a million rabbits. He cackled with delight as he watched the swarm spread out across the ice floes, like some giant furry menace that hopped and bounced toward the terrified blubbery walruses. You might wonder why Foxy wanted to be so mean to the walruses - so do I, to be honest - but who knows what really goes on inside that nasty old fox's mind?

Worse was to come! Foxy McFox didn't just spread his rabbit plague on land - the egg ship was also able to fly (or swim) underwater! And so once he'd finished his mean business at the Walrus Queendom, he made the ship dive deep beneath the ocean, and headed straight toward the Undersea Kingdom. Now, you might think this wouldn't be too much of a problem - as the Undersea Kingdom is very much 'under the sea' (hence its name) - and so any fluffy bunnies who go there couldn't possibly breathe underwater.

And this is perfectly true - bunnies *can't* breathe

underwater - unless they have miniature scuba outfits. And this is precisely the kind of task the foxes had been brought along for.

You see, packed inside the many large crates the foxes had fetched onboard were thousands and thousands of miniature scuba outfits - tiny little goggles, tiny little wetsuits, tiny little airtanks, and tiny little flippers. Ever since they'd arrived on the egg ship, the foxes had been busying themselves by putting the scuba suits on to many of the rabbits. And now they'd arrived at the Undersea Kingdom, it was time to unleash them on the King of the Undersea Kingdom, and all his aquatic subjects!

I'm sure you can imagine the scene - the King of the Undersea Kingdom had been contentedly sat on his throne, reading his morning newspaper and slurping a nice cup of tea. Everything was blissful within his kingdom, as little sea animals fanned him to keep him cool, and his royal courtiers busied themselves with their daily business. Then suddenly, amid cries of astonishment and wails of fear, all the crabs and dolphins and whales and fish and blobby, floaty aquatic thingys all fled in terror as many thousands of scuba-suited bunny rabbits came swimming toward them!

They were soon nibbling on the coral walls of the kingdom (making spires and towers crumble and fall to the seabed), and they left millions of little brown poo pellets everywhere (which turned the once beautifully clear waters all dark, murky and smelly). The King screamed like a girl as they thundered into his court, like a fluffy-but-soggy tidal wave. Within seconds they were nibbling at his throne, their squeaks echoing like a rumbling storm within the courtroom. Once more, Foxy McFox left a few of his business cards (which were of course waterproof, so that the King could read the details clearly) - as the nasty old fox knew it was just a matter of time before the King of the Undersea Kingdom could stand the bunnies, their squeaks, their poo-dollops and their nibbling no longer.

Once he had finished tormenting the King of the Undersea Kingdom, Foxy McFox headed to Queen Sheep's Farm. Her farm was renowned the world over, but not for the most pleasant of reasons. You see, Queen Sheep's Farm had a rather unpleasant occupant - an extremely revolting pig, that went by the name of Podge.

Now, Queen Sheep and her subjects had suffered a great deal over the years, as a result of that particular pig's bottom - it was very, very explosive indeed! So explosive, that Podge was known to one and all as the pooiest, ploppiest pig on the planet - which was an accolade he was very, very proud of!

So as you can imagine, the LAST thing the long-suffering Queen Sheep and her subjects needed was something like an invasion of rabbits to make their lives even more miserable. Unfortunately, that's exactly what they got! Only Podge the pig was content as the invasion unfurled; he laughed and laughed as Queen Sheep and her snooty subjects all ran about the farm in terror, as thousands of bunnies hopped after them.

After Queen Sheep's farm, Foxy McFox took the egg ship to the island of Oom-Balla-Papa-Lalla-Shaka-Manaloko. Although the island had no bunnies of its own, the islanders there *had* met rabbits before - you may recall that the Easter Bunnies' helpers had visited there in the past, to buy lots of vanilla essence for the chocolate eggs.

When the islanders saw the egg ship arrive, and watched as loads of bunnies began to tumble out of the craft's dispatch doors, they were initially very pleased to see them all. So many bunnies suggested the islanders would soon be doing a lot more business, and making lots and lots of money.

So it may come as no surprise to you to know that the islanders were soon very confused by these new, brainless little nibbling-machines. The rabbits LOOKED the same as the intelligent helper bunnies that had visited previously, but these new ones squeaked instead of speaking, and hopped around NAKED, instead of wearing smart clothing! And ate anything and EVERYTHING that came into their line of sight - including their precious and rather expensive vanilla plants. But the most concerning thing of all to the islanders was that the bunnies seemed to multiply whenever you turned away from them for a few seconds. Thousands became *hundreds of thousands* in next to no time at all.

But once again, Foxy McFox just didn't care. Cackling to himself, he threw a few more business cards from his window (which landed on one of Oom-Balla-Papa-Lalla-Shaka-Manaloko's lovely white, sandy beaches), then sped off to his next destination.

As mentioned, Foxy McFox continued this horrible plan of action for seven days. And with every passing day he got ever more ambitious with his choice of target. He dropped bunnies into twenty of the world's major cities, causing absolute chaos, carnage and riots. New York, San Francisco, London, Berlin, Paris ... they all quickly fell to the power of the bunny invasion.

The Eiffel Tower in Paris soon began to creak and wobble, thanks to the weight of all the bunnies that hopped about on its structure. Owing to

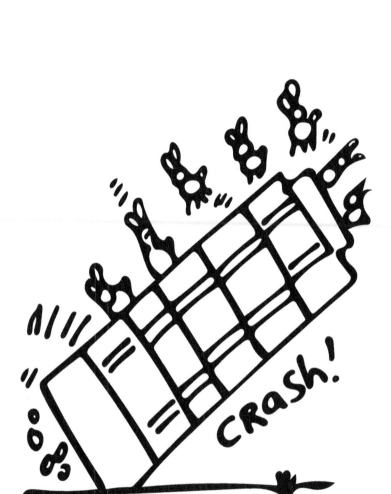

thousands of rabbits sitting on top of it, the Leaning Tower of Pisa began to lean a little too much, until it eventually crashed to the ground. The shockwave caused by millions of hopping bunnies caused the Great Wall of China to begin crumbling, and avalanches of snow to come thundering down mountains all over the world.

Foxy McFox dropped his rabbits where many of the world's leaders lived or worked - places like the White House, the Houses of Parliament, Tiananmen Square, and the Kremlin.

The one place he DIDN'T target was the country of Belgium, for two simple reasons. The first reason was that Foxy thought this little country was horrible-enough already, and didn't think millions of destructive rabbits would make much difference to the place. The second reason was chocolate; the people of Belgium do make some of the finest, scrummiest chocolate in the world (and lots of it) - and so Foxy reasoned that if he allowed his rabbits to stuff themselves with Belgian choccies they'd all get too fat and lazy, and fail to do the job he wanted them to do.

All in all, this was pretty MAD reasoning from Foxy, but the Belgian's weren't complaining. To the north, the people of Holland were getting all their cheese and wooden clogs devoured by bunnies, and the same thing was happening to the south - where the French were rapidly running out of baguettes and edible snails. To the east, the Germans had only about 37 sausages left, and the British to the west had run out of fish and chips. But the lucky Belgians managed to avoid the bunny invasion - and held on to their chocolates, too!

Foxy was very careful to attack any air bases and army camps he came across. This was to prevent anyone from sending up things like planes, rockets and missiles - anything that might cause the egg ship a bit of bother, basically.

The other thing to mention of course is that even if anyone HAD tried to attack the egg ship, it wouldn't really have done much good. You see, years earlier the Easter Bunny had fitted her flying factory with missiles, rocket launchers, cannonettes, bombs, machine guns, deflector shields, tractor beams and many, many other defences. So as well as being a factory and an aircraft, it was also an egg-shaped battleship!

Foxy knew this, of course, which is another reason why he'd arranged for all his foxy mates to tag along with him and join in the fun. Some of his crew were on permanent standby to defend the ship, if ever it came to it.

'But why had the Easter Bunny fitted so much horrible weaponry to her flying factory in the first place?' you might ask. Well, you'd have to put that question to her yourself, of course. But she WAS barking mad, as you've probably already worked out, and she was very, very precious about her Easter eggs; so it would be a fairly good guess to suggest that maybe *egg-protection* was the reason.

No-one could catch Foxy McFox! And no-one knew where he would strike next! In just seven days, Foxy McFox's bunnies had just about conquered the whole world!

The sad thing is, everyone automatically blamed *the Easter Bunny* for all that had happened. After all, it was HER egg-shaped flying factory that was seen on all the TV news programmes, and (everyone assumed) it was HER bunnies that were now taking over the world. Everyone just thought she had gone completely bonkers and caused all this herself.

"My reputation is in tatters," she tearfully said to her bunny companions, as she watched the latest news bulletins through a TV/electronics store window.

She and her helpers were still 'on the road' after they'd missed Foxy at Foxtown - and she had vowed to never return to the factory grounds until she had caught up with the cruel fox and confronted him. They were all also 'lying low'; sleeping rough in the countryside and trying to avoid unwanted attention from people like the police and the army.

Dusk was approaching, and they were currently right on the edge of some tiny, all-but-forgotten little town called Snodville. Nobody seemed to be about - there had been a 'bunny invasion' in the area three days previous, and most of the local inhabitants had evacuated to a 'secure area'. I say 'most' and not 'all', because there were still a few residents who'd refused to budge - and the Easter Bunny knew this. For this reason, she'd refused to let her bunny colleagues rest-up in the town - she didn't want them to get caught, and she didn't want anyone to pass word that they were in the vicinity.

She'd allowed some of the more cautious bunnies to slip into a couple of the town's convenience stores, so they could stock-up on some of the provisions they needed - but that was all.

The Easter Bunny was convinced that no-one would believe she wasn't responsible for all the trouble that had been caused, and that if she was caught she'd be thrown into prison. Then she would NEVER be able to stop Foxy from causing even more terror and destruction; she HAD to keep her head down, and wait until she could do something about the awful things that had happened.

The problem was, she had absolutely no idea where he would strike next. The targets for his 'bunny-bombing' all seemed so random - at 9 o'clock he might attack a major city, then two hours later he'd be offloading thousands more rabbits in some isolated little village in the middle of nowhere.

She and her group of helper bunnies watched the latest bad news unfurl on the TV, until they could watch no more. There were bunnies everywhere now - in almost every country; on many smaller islands; even on the International Space Station! They heard a rumble of thunder above and heavy rain started to come down, soaking Mildred and the bunnies to their skins. Wearily, miserably, they trudged away from the illumination of the TV store window, and went off to find some sheltered ditch that they could spend the night in.

They walked for two hours or more in the heavy rain as night fell - they shuffled out of Snodville, the small town they'd window-watched TV in, and back into the darkness of the wet, muddy and inhospitable countryside. Nobody said a word, and gloom hung over the bunny brigade as heavily as the storm clouds above their floppy-eared heads.

Suddenly, the Easter Bunny stopped in her tracks - which made all the others lurch to a halt. They felt so sorry for her, as they looked up at her bulky outline - she was absolutely soaked to the bone, and every step for her had been such a miserable trudge.

"Enough of this," she calmly announced. "We need a plan. And I think I have one."

CHAPTER FOUR

THINK LIKE A FOX

W e've been doing this all wrong," Mildred the Easter Bunny explained to her soggy bunny companions, as they stood in the middle of the dark, wet country road. "We've been traipsing round the countryside like criminals, getting soaked and weary and trying to second-guess where Foxy is going to spring up next. And WE haven't done a single thing wrong! We'll NEVER catch up with him that way, and we'll never again be able to raise our heads and say 'We are proud to be bunnies' if we don't start turning things around."

"Well, I hadn't realised we were trying to

CATCH him," said the well-built bunny named Marmaduke, warily. "I'm not sure we could take on that nasty old fox and all his sly, foxy friends. I just thought we were going to try and find him, then contact someone who's got the means to deal with him."

"I don't think anyone would believe us," replied Mildred the Easter Bunny. "I really think it's down to us, now."

"What's the plan, then?" asked the elderly Mrs Fluffywinkle, with determination. Old or otherwise, she wasn't going to be scared of Foxy McFox, after everything they'd already been through.

"Well, first - we need to get out of this bloomin' rain," smiled the Easter Bunny. She pointed to a cornfield in the west, where a small coppice of trees grew at the far end of it. "Let's get under those trees, and set up a camp. We'll be well out of sight, and out of this awful weather."

"Well, seven days are just about up," Foxy McFox chuckled to himself, from the comfort of his pilot's seat. He'd been watching images of the egg ship he was flying on the TV news, and had spent the evening chucking aloud as he saw all the bunny destruction he had caused over the past week. Things couldn't be working out better.

He called on the ship's tannoy to Clodwell, asking for a 'status report'.

"All lookin' good, boss," was the quick reply. "We've already had loads of calls and emails from people desperate to get shot of their bunnies. Most of 'em will pay any price we ask. The world leaders and the super-rich are best - they'll pay BILLIONS to get rid of the rabbits; no questions asked. And we're still knee-deep in bunnies down here, in case you want to bunny-bomb anyone else."

"Nah, I'm a bit bored of dropping rabbits on people now, to be honest," was Foxy's yawning response. "We'll only have to collect 'em all up again, when we move to Stage Three. So let's not cause ourselves too much work, shall we?" He thought for a moment. "Let's just keep hold of the remaining rabbits, and then they'll be handy for when the next stage starts. In the meantime, how are the boys gettin' on with converting all the factory machinery?"

"Not bad at all, boss," was the eager response. "We dumped all that chocolate-making gear, and installed all the new stuff that we fetched from Foxtown. It'll all be up and running in a day or so."

"Nice one," replied Foxy, with a grin. The guys had done him proud.

Clodwell spoke again; "Erm, me and the boys were wondering, boss - when ARE we movin' to Stage Three?" Foxy McFox could hear the excitement in Clodwell's voice, and heard the lick of his lips. Stage Three was going to be the part of the plan that ALL the foxes were going to enjoy best of all.

"Oh, soon enough, Clodwell," Foxy replied. "Patience, patience. Not long now."

An hour or so after leaving the country road, Mildred and her rabbit companions had set up a basic camp in the small woodland shelter. Most of the bunnies had quickly dug out shallow holes in the muddy soil there, and they reassembled in a clearing between the trees once they'd rested a short while. They weren't used to burrowing holes - after they'd been fzapped by the Easter Bunny's brain-ray, they'd all preferred the finer things in life, such as the cosy little beds in the fine cottages she had given them, back at the factory. But the comfy life they'd enjoyed seemed long-gone now, and burrowing holes for shelter was the only option for the poor, bedraggled bunnies.

"Here's the plan," began the Easter Bunny, once they were all together again. "There's no way to guess where Foxy will turn up next, so instead WE have to be CRAFTY."

"Like a fox," said Marmaduke, keen to impress.

"Exactly," she replied. "If a fox can't catch its prey by RUNNING after it, what does it do?"

"Go and grab a burger instead?" suggested a geeky young bunny named Snooks. Everybody scowled at him.

"No," answered Mildred, patiently, "it does *not* 'go and grab a burger'. It sits. And it waits."

"So ...," began a surly teenage bunny named Tabitha, who was trying to work out the plan (and sounding fairly sarcastic in the process, like most teenagers do); "you're saying that we're just going to sit ... and WAIT for the foxes to come to US?"

The Easter Bunny nodded.

"But that'll take forever," Tabitha replied, shaking her head and thinking the Easter Bunny maybe WAS as nuts as everyone seemed to think she was.

"It won't take forever if we offer the foxes some bait," replied the Easter Bunny.

"BAIT?" repeated Marmaduke. "What do you mean by 'bait'?"

"Us!" replied the Easter Bunny. "We let Foxy and the other foxes know EXACTLY where we are. That way they'll come and get us." She smiled broadly, proud of her plan. Now it wasn't just moody Tabitha who thought she was crazy.

"But then they'll come and EAT us," said Marmaduke, in disbelief.

"They'll TRY," replied the Easter Bunny. "But we'll be ready for them."

Now it was Marmaduke who was shaking his head in disbelief. "But as I said before, Ma'am - I really don't think we're capable of taking on a gang of murderous foxes. And why should they even BOTHER with us, anyway? They already seem to be getting whatever it is they want - but nobody REALLY knows what they're up to, do they? They've ruined Easter for everyone this year, but that's just the start of it; they're now on the way to ruining the world, by letting our pea-brained bunny cousins run riot everywhere - and goodness knows where it's all going to end."

The Easter Bunny smiled once more. As always, she was benign and gracious and seemed confident about everything she was saying. If nothing else, it gave some comfort to her bunny companions. "Don't worry, Marmaduke - my plan will work, and they'll come to us. Because we have something Foxy wants. We're probably the only ones in the world who know that it's Foxy who is behind all this - and I'm betting he'd rather the world didn't know the truth."

Old Mrs Fluffywinkle nodded in agreement. "Oh,

he'll come for us, alright. He won't be able to resist. But first, we need to find some way to let him find us."

"Indeed - and that's where Tabitha and Snooks come in," replied the Easter Bunny, to the bemusement of the young bunny-geek and the girly teenage grump.

The Easter Bunny thought she and her bunny colleagues were the only ones in the whole world who knew the truth about Foxy McFox, but she wasn't entirely correct. As you may recall, the Elf Doctor had briefly spoken to Foxy through one of the egg ship's windows, just before he'd dumped thousands of rabbits on to the North Pole's airstrip.

Now, you don't need me to tell you that as soon as the wave of bunnies had started hopping and bouncing toward Elf Town, the Elf Doctor had spent the rest of that particularly stressful day being very busy indeed. He whizzed about on Clarence the slug's back like a Wild West cowboy, desperately trying to herd the rabbits away from Elf Town and its enormous supplies of candy goodies and toys. The Elf Doctor knew that next Christmas could be in peril if the bunnies weren't kept under control. But as you might expect, it was just a matter of time before the bunnies became too much for a single elf and his giant slug to handle - the

mountain of bunnies grew and grew, until eventually the exhausted elf had to fall back and rouse the rest of Elf Town.

He had to wake Santa, Mrs Claus and all the elves out of their exceptionally-long slumbers (which certainly wasn't easy, as they were all in 'deep-sleep mode', and hadn't planned to wake up for at least another month). When the Elf Doctor tried to wake Santa, he thought he was in some strange dream and spent half an hour wrestling the unfortunate elf, until he was finally woken by getting a face-full of Clarence's repulsive slime-vomit (from time to time, the giant slug had the unpleasant habit of sicking-up his dinner on to people's heads, you see).

Hundreds of elves snored away as they began to get smothered by thousands and thousands of bunnies, and all-in-all it took a whole day to get every single elf awake, up, and fighting back against the endless waves of bunny invaders.

But fight back they did - for no-one is as tough and hardworking as an elf when it comes to an emergency. It took the best part of a week to gain the upper hand - and here's how they managed to control their invasion ...

Santa divided his elves into two groups - half of them had to follow the Elf Doctor's cowboy antics and 'round up the herd' of bunnies, while the other half had to come up with some form of 'holding pen'. A standard low-level cage was unsuitable, even a very large one - as the bunnies would nibble their way out of it, or simply hop over the top.

And so the elves got to work in their factory, and began building an enormous 'tube' for the rabbits to be placed into. The 'bunny tube' was designed so that new sections could be added to the top, as necessary - so, as the bunnies increased in number, the bunny tube could be increased in height.

The bunny tube grew and grew, until it was soon well above the highest spire on the highest building in Elf Town - and still the bunnies continued to multiply. Tall construction cranes and helicopters were speedily designed and assembled within the Elf Factory, so that new sections could keep on being added to the tube. It was certainly no answer to getting rid of the rabbits, but it did at least contain them and keep them away from Elf Town. For the time being at least, next Christmas was saved.

Once order was (to some degree) restored at the North Pole, the Elf Doctor finally had time to tell Santa all he knew about Foxy McFox and the egg ship's arrival earlier in the week. They assembled in the Elf Factory - also in attendance were Mrs Claus, the Elf

Wizard and a small number of senior Factory Elves. Clarence the slug was there too (seeing as the Elf Doctor was almost always perched on his back), though being a near-brainless example of giant slug he had absolutely no idea where he was, or why he was there.

None could believe at first that the sly old fox had seemingly managed to steal the Easter Egg Factory from under Mildred's nose - much like the Elf Factory, Santa knew there was nearly always someone in attendance to watch over the place.

And they were of course all horrified when they switched on the TV news, and saw the rest of the world falling to ruin as a result of the bunny invasions. But worst of all to them was the knowledge that it was actually Mildred the Easter Bunny who was taking all the blame for Foxy's foul actions!

Santa was furious; the Easter Bunny was a close personal friend, and he knew her better than just about anyone else - how *dare* the rest of the world accuse her of causing all this chaos? He went red with rage when he saw the TV news showing 'Wanted' posters of her, and then went *deep purple* with rage when the TV showed crowds of angry people, all carrying banners and calling for her to be caught and sent to prison - or much worse.

But where was she? - that was the question no-one could answer. Had Foxy done something awful to her - or was she in hiding because of all the horrible people who were now out to get her?

"We've got to put an end to all this," Santa said, as his anger began to cool and his cheeks returned to their normal colour. "Assemble the elves - the Easter Bunny needs us!"

CHAPTER FIVE

TABITHA AND SNOOKS

The two young bunnies never once stopped bickering and moaning, as the pair of them trudged all the way back to the town of Snodville.

"Why couldn't the Easter Bunny have had her 'brilliant plan' when we were here earlier?" grumbled Snooks, as the lights of the town finally appeared in the distance.

"Because she's, like, *making it all up* as she goes along," replied Tabitha, as she rolled her eyes. She couldn't sound more bored if she tried. "It's what adults do, you idiot; they make out they're 'mature' and 'responsible', and always expect us to just follow their orders like we're mindless sheep. But in reality they haven't A CLUE what they're doing. It totally sucks."

"Something you actually got right," grunted Snooks. "Still dunno why she picked us two to go and get the supplies she needs, though."

"It's obvious, you dummy," sighed Tabitha. "Well, at least in terms of why *I'm* here. I'm by far the best of all of us at getting into that electrics store on the edge of town. But as for you - I've no idea." She snorted. "Probably to 'make up the numbers', I guess."

Snooks scowled at the teenage rabbit. "Yeah, right, Tab-ee-tha," he replied, sarcastically. "Like you'd know what to look for, when you get us into that place. IF you get us into that place, I mean. The Easter Bunny needs ME to get all the parts we need, and ME to put together the microwave communicator to contact the foxes. I'm the one with the technical know-how. I'm the one with the technical *skills*. I'm the one with the deft little bunny paws, that can assemble components and install processors faster than lightning. If *anyone* is expendible, Little Miss Hey-I-Can-Pick-A-Lock, Little Miss Wall-Of-Endless-Emo-Negativity, then I'd say that someone is YOU. I mean - can you actually DO anything, other than stand around oozing your hormonal bad attitude with a face that looks like it's chewing a wasp?" Snooks smirked a precocious tooth-and-braces-filled smile at Tabitha, confident his put-downs would always be better than hers.

Tabitha groaned and slumped her shoulders. Oh! What would it take to make this geeky rabbit brat *just stop talking*?!? After two hours of his irritating, pre-teen motor-mouthing she'd just about do anything to shut him up. "Alright!" she finally said, unable to take any more. "Alright; how much? How much do I need to PAY YOU to shut up until we've got this mission out of the way?"

Snooks smirked again, looking at her in mock disgust. "I don't want your money, you panda-eyed whingebag. I just want you to admit that you - having been defeated by my superior reasoning skills - are the one who is here to 'make up the numbers' - not me."

"Oh, whatever," sighed Tabitha, just as she and Snooks simultaneously realised they'd already arrived at the edge of the town of Snodville, and were standing in front of the TV/electronics store they needed to somehow get in to.

"Oh wow," she murmured to Snooks. "You like, DO have skills after all - your endless talking creates a tedium time-warp so that we can arrive someplace without realising it."

"Just get on with breaking and entering," sighed

Snooks. "Hmm ... your mother must be so proud - to have brought up a daughter with such *classy* abilities. D'you want me to fetch you a nail-file, or something, to help you pick the door lock?"

"Nail-files are so old school, you waste of space," she groaned, before turning her attention to the locked entrance. There was no way she could have picked the door lock anyway - it was just too high. They'd need to resort to other measures, so she stood back to take a better look at the building.

"Can you climb?" she asked Snooks after a time, who shook his head with a sarcastic laugh.

"I'm a *bunny*, Tab-ee-tha," he replied, his eyes like slits. "In case you're not up on the biology of our species, I should perhaps explain that we tend to hop, not climb."

"It wasn't really a question, you fartburger," she replied, and gave him a sharp bite on his rear. He squeaked in pain and jumped skyward, landing on the shop's drainpipe.

"See?" continued Tabitha, as she studied the upper level of the outside of the building. "You CAN climb. Keep going; we need to get level with the first storey, as I've spotted an open window."

"YOU'RE supposed to be the cat-burglar," growled Snooks in response, "not me."

"I'm right behind you," she replied, as she got her first paw on the drainpipe. "So keep climbing. Or I'll bite again."

Snooks had never really climbed anything in his rather short life, but the threat of 'bitey Tabitha' spurred him on to quickly reach the first storey. Sure enough, to his right he could see that whoever had vacated the TV store had failed to completely shut one of the windows. The frame was ajar just enough for a small animal like Snooks to squeeze through - provided he could make the jump from the drainpipe to the window ledge without falling. To encourage Snooks, Tabitha called up to him.

"Falling would be kinda bad right now," she advised, in her usual bored tone. "Probably best you don't slip and fall to a messy, splattery death on the road down below."

"Why ARE teenagers so utterly irritating?" was his gritted-teeth response.

"You know, I've really no idea," she answered with a sigh, "but if you want the opportunity to grow up and find out for yourself one day, then don't slip up right now."

He didn't. Unable to hold on to the wet and slippery drainpipe much longer, Snooks had no option but to make the jump into the unknown and just hope he'd used enough force to propel him on to the window ledge. He had - but only just. His little bunny claws caught the edge of the window ledge; he hung there for a moment, before fear urged him to scamper upwards. Uncaring about whether Tabitha would also manage to make the jump, the young bunny squeezed and scrambled through the gap in the ledge and slipped inside the building.

"Yay, you made it," mumbled Tabitha, with about as much enthusiasm as a dead snail. Then, quite effortlessly compared to Snooks's desperate lunge, she gracefully twisted and swung herself on to the ledge, and followed the young rabbit inside.

Once inside, they realised they were in the upstairs apartment of the TV store-owners. No lights were on, so it took a minute or two of fumbling around in the darkness before one of them finally found the switch for a table lamp.

Now they had some light, they could see they were in somebody's extremely untidy living room. A stack of used pizza boxes was thrown in one corner. The worn, ancient sofa was covered in chunks of dried, uneaten food (pizza slices, mostly) and lots of squashed-up beer cans littered the floor. A skateboard stood in one corner, wedged against a pile of movie and videogame disks. There were unpleasant-looking posters half-hanging off stained and scuffed unpainted walls. What little furniture there was in the room looked cheap and very old, and had chunks of corners broken off, from being roughly handled in the past. The place didn't smell so good, either.

"Ewww," said Tabitha, unimpressed. "Pretty nasty in here."

"You should feel right at home," replied Snooks, snorting a laugh at her.

"Hmm; the store-owner's obviously a pretty classy guy," said Tabitha, ignoring Snooks's last comment. "Beer and pizza - what a slob. Let's go see what we can find."

They hopped from the room and on to the landing, above a stairwell that led down to the lower floor. It was faintly illuminated by moonlight coming through a hallway window - at least that meant the storm clouds were breaking up, and they'd hopefully have a dry walk back to the camp. They then hopped down the steps, until they were back at ground level once more. Following the lower hallway round, they came to another door - the back entrance to the store.

"Another locked door," observed Snooks. "And don't *bite* me this time, you weirdo." He looked at Tabitha, then back at the door's lock, in a 'this is YOUR part of the job' manner.

Tabitha sighed at Snooks, shaking her head. "You're such an embarrassment," she quipped. She then hopped on to the back of a nearby chair, which slowly tilted backwards from the force of her landing - and came to rest against the door, just beneath the lock. From here it was a simple matter for her to reach up and work on it. She casually pulled a tiny hairpin from the pink and blue dyed mohican fur atop her head, and jammed it into the lock. With a long, bored yawn and a couple of twists of the pin she had it unlocked in a matter of seconds. She turned the door handle slightly, so the door would open a fraction, then rocked back on the chair so that it wouldn't fall heavily against the now-unlocked rear entrance. A hop and a jump later, and she was making her way into the shop.

"Are you coming, or are you just gonna stand there all day admiring my coolness," she quipped to Snooks, as she ambled into the store.

There wasn't much light inside - most of it was weak and yellow and came from the streetlamps outside. The rest of the light was the glow from the TVs that sat in the store window - their screens projected the latest news to an empty town - the slobby store-owner had forgotten to switch them off. But what light they had was enough for Snooks to work with, as he hopped around the store aisles, searching for what he needed. Naturally, most of the components, tools, wire coils, screws and other bits and bobs he needed were unreachable on high shelves, and he usually needed to reluctantly beg Tabitha to get up to those higher levels and pass the supplies down to him. When I say 'pass', I do of course mean 'throw violently at Snooks', as there was very little in the way of delicacy in her actions when it came to dealing with the 'annoying brat' she felt she'd been lumbered with.

Privately, Snooks was amazed at how easily she jumped and flitted from shelf to shelf - she was as nimble as a circus trapeze-artist - though outwardly, as already shown, any hint that he was impressed by her skills would never be admitted to.

Similarly, Tabitha soon found she wasn't *completely* nauseated by the underage geek she'd been forced to work with. Once he'd got the various components he needed to create a microwave communicator, his genius began to show. He sat on the shop floor with his tools beside him, working like lightning as he assembled the many different components together; circuits and solenoids, conductors and regulators, amplifiers and digitizers - he seemingly had the ability to turn everyday, ordinary electronic gizmos into something wildly futuristic.

"All done," he announced, after about an hour of

feverish assembling.

Tabitha, naturally, wasn't going to suggest she was impressed with his electronic creation, and snorted her derision. "Way to go, Einstein - you've managed to make a hairdryer the size of an adult pig. That'll really come in handy when we need to contact the foxes. And, like ... why didn't you design it in *miniature*? It looks *stupid*."

Snooks groaned and sighed at the same time. She was right; the finished microwave communicator WAS shaped like a hairdryer, and WAS the size of an adult pig. But he kind of thought she was missing the point - he hadn't been too concerned about how it looked or how big it was, just that it would work when it was needed. "You know, Tab-eeeeee-tharrr - if you like, I could take some more of the electronics in this store and actually fashion you a brain."

"Like your enormous pig-dryer's going to work," she scoffed, shaking her head.

"It will," Snooks replied, confidently. "But seeing as I've done all the work here, now YOU'VE got to put your smaller, vacuous teen-brain to a new challenge."

"And that challenge is?" she asked, giving him one of her best 'I truly hate you, you little geek' looks.

Ignoring her, Snooks pointed to the microwave communicator and said; "How are we going to get it back to the camp?"

The answer to Snooks's question, as it turned out, wasn't too difficult for Tabitha, once she'd taken a thorough and careful look around the store. Nothing here seemed suitable for the job of getting it back to the camp in the woods, but thinking back, she soon hit on a bright idea.

"We're gonna *wheel it*," she finally replied.

"Explain," sighed Snooks.

"Unnecessary," was the reply, as Tabitha once again showed her practical talents. Without another word, she hopped off in the direction of the store's back entrance, and quickly bounded and skipped up the stairs. Snooks listened to an occasional faint bump and thump coming through the ceiling as Tabitha went about doing whatever on Earth it was that she was doing up there. All went quiet for a time, and Snooks started getting anxious in the twilight-illumination; despite his superior brain, he was still a very young bunny, after all.

Then there was a sudden 'sliding rumble' and a thump, as something in the darkened hallway came crashing down the stairs. Then silence returned. Snooks's little heart beat overtime - thrump-a-thrump-a-thrump - as he cautiously crept toward the rear entrance of the shop, and peered into the hallway.

Nothing out there. Nothing but silence.

"T-Tabitha?" he weakly called out. It was the first time he'd used her name without sarcasm.

"Boo!" growled Tabitha, making him jump out of his saggy, floppy-eared skin and causing his heart to skip a couple of beats. She'd suddenly jumped from her hiding place to one side of the doorframe, with a mean smirk on her face.

"Y-you trying to give me a heart attack?!" he bawled in her face.

"Well, it would mean a quieter walk back to the camp, for one thing," she cackled. "And I could always say the foxes got you. Anyway; look what I found - *wheels*." She glided in front of him, riding the skateboard they'd seen in the grimy lounge upstairs. "I reckon this'll do the trick."

"We've still got to get the microwave communicator on top of it," reminded Snooks, who was keen to make sure he didn't look too impressed with the skateboard. "Anyway, there's wheels in the store, you freakin' idiot - didn't you see all the shopping trolleys out front?"

"Sure, she replied, sneerily, "but I'd like to see YOU push the combined weight of a steel trolley and your enormous, oversized pig-dryer. And then there's the task of *getting* your enormous, oversized pig-dryer

on to a trolley, which I think is also probably a little beyond your abilities. A skateboard, however, is much lower to the ground, turdbrain - meaning we'll be able to get your hunk of junk on it with less difficulty."

The two bunnies glowered at one another for what seemed like an age.

"I hate you," Snooks eventually mouthed.

"I know," Tabitha replied, smirking.

However, despite their fairly obvious differences and utter, utter dislike for one another, they did manage to do exactly what Tabitha had suggested. It took much heaving and pulling - using ropes, a makeshift ramp and an awful lot of bunny brute-strength and determination - but eventually they managed to line-up the loaded skateboard so that it could be pushed out of the store's front door.

Before they could trundle off into the distance, there was still the issue of the locked front door - but as they'd already achieved so much this long evening, Tabitha saw this obstacle as just a walk in the park. All she had to do was swing up on the shelving nearest to the front door, and launch herself on to the door's lock mechanism. Holding herself in place with her hind paws, she'd twiddle the lock with a hairpin just as she'd done on the store's back door.

And that's exactly what she did - except

overconfidence let her down just then. She failed to look out for any alarm pads or wires that connected to the door - and as soon as she'd got the door ajar, a shrill, shrieking and deafening alarm was set off.

Now, this shrill, shrieking and deafening alarm woke up BEEF. *'Who's Beef?'* you may ask. Good question. Perhaps it's one Tabitha and Snooks should have asked before breaking into his store.

You see, Beef was the store-owner. A slobbish, heavy-sleeping, heavy-drinking, heavy-bellied store-owner, who liked his pizza, liked his scruffy sofa, liked his videogames and movies, and liked his beer. The one thing he DIDN'T like was when official people such as the police and the army told him to evacuate his store and home, because there was the possible risk of a bunny-invasion in the vicinity. No-one official was going to make Beef leave his own property, because then it would be at risk from looting and vandalism. And he certainly wasn't going to leave because of a possible threat from a few bunny rabbits. And so he stayed. And drank, and ate. And watched TV, and played videogames. And slept.

Downstairs, bunny rabbits were looting his store, and breaking in and out of his property - which Beef would class as acts of vandalism.

Now, the Easter Bunny's intention was to

compensate the TV and electronics store-owner - once they'd finally resolved the predicament they were currently in - though of course, if the bunnies downstairs said *'Don't worry - the Easter Bunny will pay you'* - you will probably not be surprised to hear that Beef would find this very hard to believe.

Beef had - in case you hadn't already guessed - been sleeping heavily in his bedroom all night, after an evening of sitting on his unpleasant sofa, drinking lots of beer, eating pizza, drinking lots more beer, playing videogames, drinking even more beer, and watching movies. He'd slept through the bunnies creeping and crashing about in his living room, and slept through them hopping downstairs, breaking in through the store's back door and sorting out the tools and components Snooks needed for his machine. He'd slept through the hour of Snooks assembling the machine, and had even slept through Tabitha sliding and crashing down the stairs whilst riding his skateboard. But the one thing he DIDN'T sleep through was the sound of the shrill, shrieking and deafening front door alarm.

Which is why, five seconds later, he was standing at the back door of his store, sweating and panting and glaring angrily at two bunny rabbits - who had seemingly spent the evening stealing half of his store's supplies, and were now trying to trundle them out of the front door on a skateboard. HIS skateboard.

To get down to the store in five seconds for a man as big and heavy as Beef was quite impressive. Even more impressive was the fact he'd somehow managed to load a shotgun in those same five seconds. But Tabitha and Snooks weren't too concerned about how quickly the weighty store owner had managed to achieve all this - they were more concerned about the fact he was pointing his loaded shotgun RIGHT AT THEM.

I mentioned just before that Beef would probably find it hard to believe if one of the bunnies tried to pacify him by saying; *'Don't worry - the Easter Bunny will pay you'*. This is exactly what WAS said - by Snooks. And of course, Beef was not pacified by this. Nor of course did he believe it. And of course he was pretty freaked out by talking bunnies in his store - both of whom were dressed in clothing and one of whom (Tabitha) had a mohican haircut.

And so, wailing in terror and anger, he started firing his shotgun at the bunnies. He was a lousy shot, thankfully - he'd kept the shotgun for years in case of trouble, but this was the first time he'd actually used it. He managed to blow away a shelf load of cheap radios (that Beef had on sale at the time), but missed the rabbits by a mile.

He ran at the bunnies, who were now frantically trying to push the skateboard and its load through the front door. But it wouldn't budge. A front wheel had jammed on a raised door seal on the floor, halting its progress.

"Time to ... like, get out of here, or something," said Tabitha, with almost a hint of urgency in her voice.

"Tell me about it!" wailed Snooks, who was doing most of the work in regards to pushing the skateboard.

But fortune favoured the bold that evening. As Beef ran at them, he tripped over some of the unwanted electronic components Snooks had left scattered around on the floor. Now out of control and stumbling forward, Beef slammed into the back of the microwave communicator machine, ramming it over the door's threshold and on to the road outside. With a howl and a crunching "Unfph!" sound, Beef rolled and crashed into the side of the door frame, stunning himself. Tabitha and Snooks jumped and clung on to the skateboard's cargo, as it wheeled and swerved and turned and twisted and almost toppled-over as they were forcibly ejected from the shop - but eventually the skateboard stabilised and started rolling down the road.

"Keep it moving!" yelled Snooks to Tabitha. "If it

stops rolling now, we won't have the strength to push it and we'll just grind to a halt."

"On it already," Tabitha sighed. She was now trotting behind the skateboard, giving its load an occasional push to keep it in motion as it trundled down the road. Thankfully for the two bunnies, the highway ran pretty flat - which would make their return journey to the woodland base all the easier.

Snooks hopped down beside Tabitha, from where he'd been holding on to the microwave communicator. "You know, Tabitha - we make a pretty good team, you and me - despite you being such a teenage whingebag."

"No we don't, fartbreath," she groaned, rolling her eyes and refusing to accept his compliment. "I just make you look good, as you crawl around in the afterglow of my awesomeness."

So once again two hours of bickering and arguing ensued, as they wheeled the skateboard and the microwave communicator out of town, and into the welcoming darkness of the countryside.

CHAPTER SIX

ELVES TO THE RESCUE!

As soon as the 'bunny situation' at the North Pole had been stabilised, Santa had wasted no time in assembling his elves, for what would most likely be their most daring adventure yet. Actually, for most of the elves it would be their FIRST EVER adventure, as life for the elves over the past six hundred years or so had generally been about making toys and presents for kids - and that was about it.

But there *had* been one fairly recent Christmas adventure - where Santa had gone a bit bonkers, and it had been left to Clarence the slug to save the day - so the mass of assembled elves weren't entirely new to this kind of thing. Standing beside Santa was Mrs Claus (who was as dependable as ever), along with the Elf Wizard and the Elf Doctor (who, naturally was still sat atop Clarence the slug).

"Right, elves," began Santa, as he addressed them in the heart of the Elf Factory, "here's the situation as best I see it. We are facing an unknown foe, who appears to be intent on causing worldwide panic by distributing millions of wild bunny rabbits at specific targets across the globe. I say 'unknown', yet it is our firm belief that it is none other than the sly and conniving Foxy McFox who is behind all this - but it would be wrong for us to make any kind of definite conclusion at this stage. We must be prepared for any eventuality. I will now pass over to the Elf Wizard, who will enlighten you further on our specific plan of action."

The Elf Wizard, who was standing to Santa's left, stepped forward. As always, he was wearing his wizard's pointy hat and wore spangly, star-shaped sunglasses. With a twirl of his magic wand, he made an impressive-looking, three-dimensional image of the Earth appear in front of the elves, in order to help them understand the plan. He pointed at various places on the 3D map as he spoke, and sounded somewhat like a stern military commander, as he passed on the instructions. Normally he sounded like a bit of a cool and dreamy hippy, but I guess the urgency of the situation made him pull his socks up.

"Fellow elves, we have today successfully repelled a bunny attack 'here' - at the North Pole. Our tracker elves indicate a similar attack was also launched nearby, at the Walrus Queendom of Lady Karacas - though we do not know at this stage how well the walruses have fared. A small team will be sent there, to determine what assistance we can give. All remaining elves will be divided into three separate groups, to fulfill other operations."

A 3D graphic of the elves appeared in front of them, which was colour-coded so all elves knew what their roles would be. The Elf Wizard continued. "A third of you are to remain at the Elf Factory, making and assembling the large tube sections that successfully captured the bunnies that attacked us. You factory elves will come under my command. Another third of you will act as a supply convoy - delivering the tube sections to destinations across the globe in an attempt to imprison all the invading rabbits. The convoy group will come under the command of Santa, seeing as he is something of an expert in regards to delivering packages at high speed across the globe. The third team - led by the Elf Doctor - will be a special

expedition - to locate the Easter Bunny and any of her intelligent helper bunnies, if they can be located. There will also be a final, much smaller communications team, remaining at the North Pole - comprised of Mrs Claus and a couple of the older elves - who will be there to liaise with all the three larger teams. Mrs Claus will also contact the world's leaders, in an attempt to assure them that the bunny invasions are not an act of war by the Easter Bunny."

The Elf Wizard stepped back, allowing Santa to finalise the meeting. "Thank you, Elf Wizard," he said. "Now - any questions?"

"You're not going to go messing about with giant slugs again, are you?" asked one rather cheeky elf (called Egbert), who pointed his question at the Elf Doctor. "Didn't work out too well last time, from what I recall."

"And what's wrong with Clarence?!" screeched the Elf Doctor in response. "He did remarkably well in the end, you may recall."

"I'm just saying, that's all," replied Egbert, with a shrug. "Can't send a slug to do an elf's job, now, can you? You tried that before - thinking your pet slug could do Santa's job - and it was almost a bloomin' disaster."

"Clarence can do ANYTHING an elf can do -

and better," protested the Elf Doctor, who was deeply offended that his beloved slug was taking such verbal abuse.

"Erm - no they can't," the elf responded, matter of factly. "Can't make toys, can they? Can't wear green tights, or pointy little shoes that curl up at the ends. Can't do ANYTHING, when you think about it - apart from eat vegetables, slither around and leave slime everywhere for others to clean up."

The Elf Doctor was turning purple in his rage, but Santa intervened. "Now, now - this isn't the time for pretty arguments. I'm sure Clarence will play his part in all this, just as he did when I was - ahem - a little unwell."

"Just didn't want that slug to mess things up," mumbled Egbert. "Only tryin' to help."

Ignoring the unwanted debate with the grumbling elf, Santa addressed all those assembled one final time. "Now - you all have your duties, and we must ensure we can do all we can to assist the Easter Bunny in this horrendous set of affairs, and to try and help put things right. Work hard in your tasks, and the very best of Christmassy luck to you all." And with that, he bade them all gather into their separate groups, and commence their missions.

The elves got things underway. First task of course was to see if the Walrus Queendom needed any assistance - perhaps unsurprisingly, they did.

The lands of Lady Karacas had been under siege by bunnies for a week now. Elves wearing jet packs flew above her realm and found the once brilliantly white, snow-covered Walrus Queendom had been turned an unpleasant smeary brown colour, thanks to the countless tons of rabbit droppings that had been dolloped everywhere. Rabbits of all shapes, shades and sizes hopped about unfettered, nibbling on anything and everything. There wasn't really much in the way of vegetation for the rabbits to eat, but what had once grown there - mosses, seaweeds and lichens and such - was all gone now.

There was an enormous, shifting mound of blubber at one end of the realm - moving in closer, the elves could see it was the walruses, who were gathered together in a miserable-looking cluster at the edge of the ice floes. They were being terrorised by an endless number of mindless bunnies, who contentedly hopped and jumped all over them.

"Save us!" wailed Lady Karacas, as the flying scout elves hovered low over the walruses, "they're driving us insane!" She'd managed to raise her head through a carpet of rabbits, that all-but smothered her and her walrus companions.

"Swim out into the water!" suggested the elf in charge, who yelled into a megaphone. "That should make them hop off you."

"We can't!" she bawled in response. "They just jump back on us as soon as we bob our heads out of the sea! And we're terrified of squashing them with our blubbery bellies!"

"Understood, Your Majesty," replied the flying elf, who reported in to the communications team back in Elf Town. Within an hour Mrs Claus had organised the first shipment of tube sections to be sent to the Walrus Queendom, and the containment of the wild bunnies began.

The elves in jet packs lowered themselves to the ground, and began to lure the hordes of rabbits away from the walruses. They laid a trail of fresh carrots and lettuce in the direction of the containment tubes, and were soon rounding up the bunnies in the same way cowboy ranchers herd up their cattle.

The elves worked fast and efficiently, stacking the containment tubes higher and higher as the number of rounded-up rabbits grew and grew. It took a whole day, but eventually the elves were able to call in to Elf Town and announce that the situation was - to some extent - under control.

As you can imagine, the walruses' gratitude was immense, and they wanted to assist in any way they could.

"Spread the word," suggested the elves. "Your links to the aquatic world are better than ours. Send messages to the orcas, and to the dolphins, the sea lions and anyone else who you think can help. The Undersea Kingdom and the isolated islands of the world may all be in need of help. Tell them the Easter Bunny is not responsible for all this, and that any sightings of Foxy McFox or the flying egg ship he has stolen must be relayed back to us."

Without another word, Lady Karacas led the walruses out to sea, where they did all the elves had asked. Lord Conguito, ruler of the orcas was informed in this way and he soon spread word amongst the whales of what had happened. The message spread from species to species; the sea lions told the dolphins, who in turn told the porpoises. The porpoises passed it on to the fish, who told all to the crustaceans. And so on, and so forth.

Thanks to the walruses and the other aquatic creatures, the elves soon discovered the Undersea Kingdom had shared a similar fate to the Walrus Queendom, and heard of the thousands of scuba-tanked rabbits that were nibbling the aquatic realm into nothingness. In response, scuba-tanked elves were dispatched, along with specially-adapted containment tubes. And soon the Undersea Kingdom was also set free.

And as the word spread, so too did the elves. They moved south, to the first of the lands inhabited by men, women and children, and with them came their containment tubes, and all their new-found skills in herding up the bunnies. But most importantly they fetched their message; that the Easter Bunny had nothing to do with all that had happened.

Santa's supply division rapidly deployed all that was needed for the elves to halt the bunny invasions wherever they were discovered, while the Elf Doctor's expedition hunted high and low for the Easter Bunny.

The fightback had begun.

CHAPTER SEVEN

BACK TO THE EGG SHIP

"Never, EVER send me on another mission with that GEEK," scowled and growled Tabitha to Mildred the Easter Bunny, as she glared darkly at Snooks.

"I could say the same about YOU, you freakin' idiot!" responded Snooks.

"Nonsense!" chortled the Easter Bunny in gleeful response, "you two were obviously PERFECT for one another - just as I suspected. I see before me a magnificent-looking microwave communicator - which is exactly what we needed - and only you two working so well together could have made this happen!"

Mildred told all the other bunnies that Tabitha and Snooks were to be congratulated - and the assembled bunnies gave them both a round of applause.

"Tabitha and Snooks deserve a well-earned rest for their achievements," said Mildred, "but for the rest of us it's time to get to work!" She gave instructions to her bunny helpers in regards to what they had to do next, and they set about their tasks.

First, the microwave communicator had to be taken to a high spot - so that it's antennae could send and receive microwave signals. So the helpers all heaved and pushed the machine up a small hill near the woods where they were camped, until Mildred was satisfied it was where it needed to be.

Dawn was starting to break - which helped them in terms of being able to see what they were doing, but also made them easier to spot. Don't forget that the Easter Bunny and her helpers were now classed as 'Most Wanted', and that police and army units would be on the lookout for them. But for now they were preoccupied with getting the machine ready, so that a message could be sent to Foxy McFox, and that was all that mattered.

Soon enough, the microwave communicator was in place, and Mildred was ready to send a signal.

"How does it work, Ma'am?" asked Marmaduke, as the Easter Bunny twiddled a few dials and pressed a few switches on the side of the device.

"Oh, it's easy-enough, really," she replied. "You've just got to get the wavelength at the right level, then the microwave communicator in the egg factory will spark into life and pick up the signal."

"Won't someone else hear it, and use it to track us down?" he asked.

"Oh, no - it doesn't work like that," she replied. "If it worked like an ordinary communication device - such as a phone - then yes, I daresay someone could use it against us. But there are only three machines in the world that can send and receive these signals - the one in front of us, the one at the egg factory, and the one at the North Pole, that Santa Claus uses to keep in touch with me on occasion."

Marmaduke suddenly had an idea. "So, what you're saying is - now that we've got this machine, we could actually CONTACT Santa and the elves, and ask them to help us out?"

The Easter Bunny thought for a moment, before her face lit up in realisation. "Goodness me, you're absolutely right! Well done, Marmaduke - I hadn't thought of that! I've been so preoccupied with wanting to get back at that scoundrel Foxy McFox, that it never occurred to me that we could also contact the North Pole. As soon as I've confronted that rogue of a fox, we can get in touch with the elves and ask them for assistance, if needs be."

"Erm ... shouldn't we ask them BEFORE we go up against all those foxes?" suggested Marmaduke hopefully, who still didn't think a group of fluffy bunnies could take on a gang of murderous foxes. "I reckon they'll be pretty good in a fight, those elves, and it'd be great to have them on our side."

"No, no," replied the Easter Bunny, firmly. "This is OUR fight, Marmaduke - and OUR responsibility to put things right. Besides, from what I saw on those TV bulletins we were watching last night, it appears as if the North Pole is very busy dealing with its OWN bunny problems at the moment, thanks to Foxy's wickedness."

Although his fall at the entrance to his shop had briefly knocked him out, Beef the store-owner was now very much awake - and VERY angry. Once he'd righted himself, he'd looked around the store to see how many items had been taken by Tabitha and Snooks - the answer didn't please him. He'd been made a fool of, by two bunny rabbits - two *talking* bunny rabbits - and that meant he'd have to do something about it.

As dawn rose, he looked around outside the front of his store. The town of Snodville still looked a ghost-town - there was no-one (and no bunnies) to be seen. He glanced at the TVs in his store front window - they still showed endless news bulletins about the bunny invasions across the world. Beef noticed there was an 'information' number running across the bottom of the screen. He took a note of it, and went back inside to make a phone call.

"Uh, yeah," he grunted to the telephonist who took his call. "The name's Beef. I run a store on the outskirts of Snodville." The person on the other end of the line began to write down details, and to ask questions - to which Beef was more than happy to give answers to. His answers weren't strictly accurate, as Beef intended to try and make some money out of the situation - but they were close enough to the truth to possibly cause some problems for the Easter Bunny.

"Some of those freaky Easter rabbits you been talkin' about on TV been makin' trouble for me last night," continued Beef. "There were hundreds of them, right here - in my home, an' in my store. Attacked an' nearly killed me, they did. Emptied out half my store of its provisions, and fair wrecked the place. Gonna cost me a lot of money to put everythin' right. I'm lyin' here all beat up and whatnot, an' those crazy rabbits are

out there raising hell. Just don't seem right." The telephonist took all this down, then asked Beef where he thought they might be now. "Think they headed out east," he replied. "Down along Main Street and on to the highway out to the countryside. Hard to tell, what with them all attackin' me and stuff, but there's only one road in and out of Snodville, and you can be sure they took it. Reckon you should send someone out there."

"Right," said the Easter Bunny, "let's give it a try."

The microwave communicator hummed louder and louder as it sparked into life. A line of blue lights on a side panel flickered with activity as the microwave signal began to feed from the machine's antennae. It would be sent skywards, bouncing off the hundreds of satellites that orbited the Earth, and would break down into tiny, tiny particles so that the transmission could not be read by anything other than another microwave communicator machine.

Minutes passed, as everyone held their breath. The helper bunnies pressed close in a circle around the device. Snooks was too excited to rest and wriggled his way through the rabbit-crowd, to be beside the machine in case his technical skills were needed. The machine continued to hum, the tone of its drone getting ever higher as the microwave transmission reached its peak. Then suddenly the line of flickering blue lights turned a bright and solid red - to indicate the transmission was being received by another machine.

"It's working! It's working!" squeaked Snooks to the Easter Bunny, as he hopped on the spot in his excitement.

"Someone's listening, that's for sure," said Marmaduke, as he looked at the solid red line of lights on the side panel. To him they looked ominous - red was never a reassuring colour, he thought to himself. Reminded him of danger, like red traffic lights ... and the colour of fox fur.

"Shall we try a little verbal communication?" said the Easter Bunny. "To see who's on the other end of the line?" She picked up the microphone earpiece Snooks had connected to the machine, and placed it on her head. "Hello? Is anyone there? This is the Easter Bunny speaking."

There was a pause and a crackle on the line as she waited for a response, as well as a little bit of muffled laughter. Eventually a snidey, unpleasant-sounding voice responded - a voice she recognised all too easily. It was Foxy McFox.

"Hello, Mildred - what can I do for you?"

"Well, obviously there's a GREAT DEAL you can do for me," she briskly replied, "starting with the immediate retrieval of all those millions of rampaging bunnies you've had the stupidity to scatter across the globe."

Foxy chuckled. "Mildred, my dearest - you know I'm not likely to do that," he replied. "And I bet you haven't got a clue why I let them all run riot in the first place."

"Oh, no doubt it's all down to some deranged, lunatic scheme of yours, McFox," she replied tersely, "but to be frank I've absolutely no interest in why you did it. But suffice to say I'm NOT happy about what you've done, and I very much intend to make you stop doing whatever it is you're doing."

There was wild laughter on the other end of the phone. "Did you hear that, boys?" cackled Foxy to his foxy mates, who were listening in on the conversation. "Mildred's not happy with us." There was further laughter, before he addressed the Easter Bunny directly once more, speaking mock-apologetically. "Sorry, Mildred, my dear - do go on. Me an' the boys were just having a bit of a giggle, there."

"I'm glad you find it all so amusing, McFox," she answered. "Don't you realise the devastation you've caused? Not only have you destroyed Easter across the

entire world, you've also destroyed homes and people's lives and goodness knows what else ... and to top it all the blame is resting on MY shoulders!" There was rib-splitting hilarity at the other end of the line now, as Foxy and his friends all rolled about the floor of the egg factory, screaming with laughter. It took Foxy a couple of minutes to calm down a little, before he was able to speak once more.

"I-I'm sorry, Mildred," he giggled, "I really am. You're quite right - I really have been a very naughty boy." His giggling subsided a little, as he started to regain composure - and sounded more serious all of a sudden. "But the fact is, Mildred, I have a plan underway. One that will change EVERYTHING. And no-one can stand in my way."

"I'd like to know more about this plan," the Easter Bunny replied. "If I'm to be blamed for it, I DESERVE to be told what it is. Face-to-face."

"Face-to-face?" replied Foxy, warily. "Sorry, Mildred, but that'd mean me telling you where I am - and anyone could be listening right now."

"You KNOW this is a secure line," she replied. "But if you're afraid of anyone knowing your location, YOU come to ME, instead - if that will make you feel any better."

"Could still be a trap," he snapped in response.

"What's in it for me?"

"I'M in it for you," she replied. "Me plus all my helper bunnies. We deserve to be told what you're up to, because I daresay all our fates depend on it. And we're too proud to spend our lives hiding from the rest of the world. If you're not the coward I think you are, you will pick us up and show us what you are up to. It's simple-enough to trace our location - just find the source of our transmission."

"I've already done that," he replied, with a crafty chuckle. "The screen in front of me says you're holding up in some woodland, a few miles east of a grubby little town called Snodville."

"So you know how to use my factory's scanning equipment, she responded. "Very good - that will save me the time explaining it to you. Now all you have to do is come and pick us up."

"You do realise that foxes tend to be fairly inhospitable to their guests," said Foxy. "Especially nice and juicy, edible, rabbity guests? I can't vouch for your safety."

"Oh, I've no doubt you and your scoundrels will ensure your despicable reputations will be retained," she answered. "But we care not what our fate is - only that we first see for ourselves what your foul scheme is - so that we can pass into the next world knowing the reason for our demise."

"Very well," shrugged Foxy. "But don't say I didn't warn you. If you want to be eaten, that's your business - you know what us foxes are like; we do like a bit of bunny from time to time! But in return I'll keep my end of the bargain - we'll pick you up and I'll show you what my little plan is, just like you asked. And you never know - you might even think it's a brilliant idea! Me an' the boys do, anyway. And we've made a few changes to the place since you were here last, which you may be interested in."

"Not another word," she replied bluntly, refusing to be drawn into the unsavoury actions of foxes. "We shall await your arrival." And with that, the Easter Bunny turned off the microwave communicator.

"So now we wait," she announced to the assembled bunnies.

"Ooh, I'm gonna get eaten," whimpered Marmaduke, before fainting.

An hour or so passed, and the bunnies sat in an assembled cluster in the middle of the coppice. The sun rose higher in the morning sky, and nothing but the occasional chirp of birdsong or buzz of insects disturbed the peace and quiet. All the helper bunnies were very apprehensive, as you might expect - waiting to be picked up by a gang of cruel foxes seemed completely non-sensical to everyone.

Not a word was said as they huddled together, but they passed worried glances amongst themselves. The Easter Bunny, by contrast, looked calm, serene and relaxed - the others wondered whether she'd meant the words she'd said to Foxy on the communicator - all that talk of not caring what her fate was (or theirs, for that matter). Many of them wondered whether she'd now gone COMPLETELY MAD (just as others had suspected she'd always been pretty doolally anyway). But they ALL just hoped she knew what she was doing - for their sakes, as well as her own.

The rabbit congregation were circled by trees - so could not be seen from the highway that passed the small patch of woodland in which they sat. But they were visible from above, so the flying egg ship (when it arrived) would be able to spot them, and land in the clearing to pick them up.

And soon enough they did get some company - but it wasn't who they were expecting.

The Special Operations team closed in on the group of bunnies sat huddled amongst the trees. Dressed in camouflage gear and with their faces smeared in black polish, the army soldiers were virtually invisible against the woodland background they were now steathily creeping through.

They were of course there in response to Beef's phonecall to the information line he'd called about an hour earlier. As day broke it quickly became clear that if any bunnies had travelled east from Snodville, they must surely be hiding out in this patch of woodland - as there was nowhere else to hide on the eastern highway for many, many miles.

The fact that the bunnies hadn't heard the Special Ops team approaching was an indicator of how good these soldiers were - bunnies ears are pretty long and this allows them to hear the slightest noise (as I'm sure you know), so the troops did well to reach the edge of the clearing without being detected. Once the troops were all in position, their Commander gave the silent instruction to 'intercept' the bunnies. The plan here wasn't to injure the rabbits, but to capture them, and for this task they'd all been supplied with net guns.

The poor bunnies had no warning, and no chance of escape. The soldiers' net guns were virtually silent when they were fired - and propelled large, weighted nets at the rabbits, that wound and twisted around them all, pinning them to the ground. There was a great deal of shocked wailing and screaming as you can imagine, but ultimately there was nothing at all the bunnies could do except cower on the floor, wrapped up inside their webs of unbreakable nets like trapped insects. Seconds later, the frightened bunnies were all looking up at the painted faces of a platoon of soldiers that had seemingly come out of nowhere.

The troops were amazed - they'd never seen or heard anything quite like the helper bunnies; these funny-looking rabbits were all fully attired in clothing, and protested wildly about the manner in which they'd been captured. They were of course NOTHING like the hordes of dumber wild bunnies the soldiers had been trying to round-up in the days prior to this one.

Of greatest interest to the soldiers of course was Mildred the Easter Bunny; being so much larger than the other rabbits, she caught the Commander's attention straight away.

"Well, well - looks like we bagged the ringleader," he grunted to the other soldiers, with a grim smile. "Sheesh - look at the size of her! There'll be medals in this for all of you, boys."

But just then there was a whoosh of cyclonic air as some huge and powerful aircraft blasted its thrusters downward from its position above the treetops. The air blast sent the soldiers flying, knocking them off their feet and blowing them back to the cover of the woodland edge. Some of the faster soldiers ditched their net guns, pulled out their hand weapons and fired at the enormous vessel that hovered above the tree canopy, but bullets seemed to have no effect on the aircraft. The flying vessel appeared to have a protective force field, that ricocheted the bullets, making them bounce off in all directions.

The weighted nets kept the bunnies pinned beneath the huge aircraft that hovered above them, and the powerful air blast from its engines made breathing very difficult for the captured bunnies. But soon a glowing blue beam shone from the underside of the ship, which immediately sucked them up into the bowels of the craft. The soldiers continued to shoot bullets at the ship - but once the bunnies had all disappeared inside it, the craft returned fire on the troops. This sent them diving for cover, retreating further into the woodland - and by the time they'd mustered the strength to return in numbers to the clearing, the flying vessel was long gone.

CHAPTER EIGHT

A MEATY EASTER

"Well, well - looks like I arrived just in the nick of time!" Foxy McFox and his foxy cronies stood laughing over the still-netted Mildred and her group of bunny helpers.

"I had the situation perfectly under control," Mildred replied frostily, as she refused to catch his beady little eyes glaring at her.

"Ooh, did you, now?" chuckled Foxy, with a horrid nasal cackle. "You could've fooled me." He circled the trapped rabbits, eyeing them all and licking his lips.

They were all in the flying egg factory's 'tractor

beam' room. Normally the tractor beam was used to pick up cargo loads - supplies of sugar, cocoa, and so on. This was the first time the cargo had been tangled nets full of bunnies.

Foxy McFox continued talking. "Looked to me like you and your tender, juicy-looking followers were all about to be turned into that army squadron's *lunch*. Still, there's plenty of time for SIMILAR, later. I doubt those troopers will thank me for nicking their midday meal, but that's life."

The Easter Bunny struggled in her net, as she tried to get out of her bindings. "I very much doubt they had the intention of digesting us," she replied with a dismissive sniff. "Not everyone's as murderously keen as you, you know, when it comes to rabbit meat. Anyway, are you going to help us out of these things, or what?"

"Hmm - I dunno. Are you going to behave yourselves?" asked Foxy, warily.

"Of course," she replied. "We're bunnies; it is impossible for us to do otherwise."

"Oh, I'm not so sure that you're all as 'sweet and innocent' as you'd lead me to believe - but I'll take a chance on it, seeing as you know you're all being watched every second by my hungry companions. Besides - there's nowhere you can go, anyway - I've parked the egg ship in the middle of the Gobi Desert - there's nothing but sand for hundreds of miles."

Foxy gestured to his gang of foxy mates, who crowded round the nets and drooled ravenously at the captured rabbits. "All right, lads," he said, "let them loose, for now. But WATCH them, and keep them all close together. Anyone out of line, or anyone dragging their feet - you've my full permission to eat 'em, on the spot."

A minute or two later, all the bunnies were back on their feet, stretching out sore and cramped limbs. They looked around timorously at their captors - there must be fifty foxes at least on the ship - and that was just the hungry-looking ones surrounding them.

"No way out," gulped Marmaduke to himself.

"Care to go for a little walk?" Foxy asked the Easter Bunny, with a false smile and a leading gesture of his paw. "I know you're all DYING to see what I've been up to."

She replied as she stretched out the last of the stiffness in her back. "As that was the sole purpose of this meeting - yes, I *would* like to take a look."

The group left the tractor beam room, and took a long, curving corridor that led to the main factory workplace; Foxy and The Easter Bunny were at the front of the procession, with the helper bunnies following closely behind, and the gang of slavering foxes taking the rear. Mildred came across plenty of wild bunnies as soon as she entered the corridor - as always, the innocent little things were mindlessly hopping about, paying no attention to anyone else.

"As you can see, they're everywhere," commented Foxy, as they passed a cluster of brown little bunnies. "Not that that's a problem for us - the more the merrier, as they say. But how DO you keep their numbers down?"

"You can't," replied the Easter Bunny, sharply. "Which is precisely why I've taken great care over the years to ensure their numbers don't increase to an unacceptable level. And you've managed to undo those efforts in less than a week."

"Oh, don't you worry your pretty little head," Foxy answered with a cruel, knowing smile, "I'll soon get their numbers down." He nodded ahead, to the huge, dome-shaped room that now lay dead ahead. "Ah - here we are, at the main factory."

The throng of bunnies and foxes spilled out into the vast, cathedral-like production centre. As before, there were wild bunnies absolutely everywhere - sitting on the tops of machinery, and hopping along lengths of pipes and conveyor belts. The foxes who were already within the enormous workplace didn't seem to mind them, though - they were all busying themselves with whatever it was they were doing to the workings of the machinery.

Mildred and the helper bunnies could see immediately that the foxes had been busy changing and converting things; gone were the chocolate-carrying pipes and tubes that had once led from the kitchen - these had now been replaced by clunky-looking pipework that led from the bottom of an immense, metallic structure in the middle of the factory. This structure looked like an inverted cone - it was wide and open at the top, and tapered down to a slim base, from which the new pipes streamed out in all directions. A circular device, that resembled a giant hamster wheel, was attached to the side of the structure.

And there was no sign of the millions of chocolate Easter eggs she and her helpers had made prior to Foxy stealing the egg ship; the pyramid of eggs that had reached almost to the ceiling had completely disappeared.

But worst of all for the bunnies were the huge vats of bubbling liquids that Foxy had installed. These enormous tanks were everywhere, and full of evil-looking chemicals - glowing, bright pink and green fluids, that swirled and hissed and gave off a foul stench.

Mildred could see shapes moving around inside the tanks. She got closer to one, to peer through the murky gunk inside - and almost jumped out of her saggy, furry skin when a demented-looking bunny suddenly swam into view. There were many more in the tank - hundreds it seemed. The helper bunnies peered into some of the other tanks, and saw more of the same.

"W-what are these?" asked Mildred. "What have you done to those bunnies?"

"Oh, they're all fine," smiled Foxy, enigmatically. "Just a little experiment of mine. I call them 'Plan B'; 'B' for bunnies. 'B' for backup."

He distracted the Easter Bunny with a question, before *she* had any more questions of her own. "Anyway, Mildred - what do you think?" Foxy raised his arms triumphantly, and spun on his heels as he looked around in wonder at what he'd created.

"Just what on Earth do you think you've done to my factory?" she scowled in response.

He smiled at the Easter Bunny, ignoring her obvious anger. Now it was time for Foxy to reveal his ultimate plan, and he was going to enjoy every second of what would follow.

"Oh, I've done QUITE A LOT to it, actually," he began, "as you can see. Well, I needed to, didn't I -

for what I've got planned. As I said before, Mildred - you really needn't worry yourself about the rabbits that've spread all over the world in the past week - because me and the boys are just about to go and collect them all up. Every single last one of them."

The Easter Bunny asked him to explain things further. He was happy to oblige.

"It's like this, you see, Mildred - over the past week, I've made arrangements with oodles and oodles of countries all around the world, to help them get rid of their very unexpected and very unwanted rabbit problems. The world's leaders all sounded very grateful to hear that we were happy to help out, and have already paid us a small fortune in advance for our services. And naturally, they've no idea that the bunny exterminators they've hired are also the ones who caused the bunny invasions in the first place! My foxy mates are all ready to fly to the four corners of the planet, to round up all those floppy eared critters, and soon the world's rabbit problem will just be a bad memory."

"So you just created a bunny invasion to make lots and lots of money," said Mildred, who was trying to get her head around Foxy's seemingly insane plan, "and now you've done that, you'll sort out all the trouble you've caused?"

"Of course," replied Foxy, "it would be wrong not to, wouldn't it?"

"But what about all the billions of bunnies?" she asked. "What happens to them? Have you got somewhere you can put them all?"

Foxy and his gang started cackling at this question. The cackles turned to chuckles, which then turned to howls of cruel laughter. Mildred and her helpers couldn't see anything to laugh about, and didn't like the cruel tone of their hilarity.

"Of course I've got somewhere to put them all!" chuckled Foxy, his ribs aching from all the laughter. "We're going to bring them back here. And then I'll make 'em all nice and snug and comfy - inside my RABBIT PIES and tins of RABBIT STEW!"

Mildred and the helper bunnies wailed in terror at this revelation. So THAT was Foxy's plan! Make billions of rabbits - then turn them into food!!!

"That's utterly horrid!" said Mildred in revolted disgust. "You really are the most BEASTLY, murderous fox I've ever had the misfortune of encountering!"

"Aw, thank you very much," beamed Foxy McFox, who was still cackling. "I do try to please. I'm going to be so rich, Mildred - an' it's all down to you!"

"B-but what about all the chocolate eggs we

made?" said Mildred. "And what about all those poor children, who were so looking forward to their Easter gifts?"

"Aw, don't worry yourself about all that either, Mildred," he replied with mock-kindness. "I've thought about all the little kiddies, too." A sly grin once again crept across his face. "You may have noticed I had to get rid of your mountain of chocolate eggs - because they were disgusting, in my opinion. But don't worry - eggs are still on the menu, and everyone's still gonna get one. If you look around at all the new pipes and machinery we've installed, you'll see that I've converted part of the factory into what you might call an 'alternative' Easter egg production line - one that doesn't need to use all that nasty chocolate you're so fond of making. We got rid of your kitchen, and all your cooking ingredients and other stuff, and stuck in the GIANT MINCING MACHINE instead."

He pointed to the giant, metallic cone in the centre of the room. "You may notice it's got a giant hamster wheel on the side - this is so that it can be powered by hundreds of bunnies, endlessly running round and around. Quite eco-friendly, when you think about it."

"Giant m-mincing machine?" asked Mildred, fearfully. "W-what do you need one of those for?"

Foxy rolled his eyes, as if the answer was obvious. "Come on, Mildred - think about it! The mincing machine is what all the bunnies are going to be THROWN INTO! And - after they've been thrown into it - what comes out the other end will all get squeezed through the new pipes and put straight into our delicious, BUNNY-FLAVOUR EASTER EGGS! So now all the little kiddies can have a meaty Easter, instead of a chocolatey one - they'll love it!"

The Easter Bunny almost fainted at this last horrific announcement from Foxy. Billions of bunnies, created just so they can be fed into Foxy's mincing machine. And meaty Easter eggs, made out of real bunnies - could anything be so ghastly?! Her head spun as she struggled to take in such evil.

"You've utterly destroyed Easter!" she shrieked, horrified at the sheer wickedness of his mad scheme.

"Aw, no I haven't," he replied with a mad and evil glare, "I've just made it tastier!"

As he'd been talking, the Easter Bunny and her helpers hadn't noticed that foxy's gang had slowly but surely closed in around them, so that now they were squeezed into a small and terrified cluster. The bunnies squeaked and whimpered in fear as many sets of sharp, gnashing teeth snarled closer and closer.

"What is it you intend to do with us, you

monstrous fiends?" demanded the Easter Bunny.

"What do you think?" replied Foxy, with all trace of his mock-friendliness now long gone. "We need to test out the mincing machine - so you bunnies can be the guinea pigs!"

And with that, Mildred and her helpers were viciously grabbed by Foxy's helpers, and carried off toward a new, iron stairwell they had installed. This led to the top of the mincing machine - but no further.

"Bung some of the wild bunnies into the hamster wheel," ordered Foxy to some of his mates, "let's get the grinder started."

About two hundred of the wild rabbits were scooped up and thrown on to the huge wheel attached to the mincing machine. They automatically began hopping, running and jumping around; a couple of minutes later, the giant wheel began to turn.

The Easter Bunny and her helpers had by now all been dragged or carried to the top of the iron stairwell by the foxes. Wailing, they all peered in terror into the huge mouth of the mincing machine, and watched helplessly as the rotating hamster wheel began to turn its cogs and razor-sharp blades.

Some of the bunnies prayed, or said their goodbyes to their colleagues. Others just closed their eyes and silently wept.

"You really are a monster!" the Easter Bunny tearfully shouted at Foxy, as he watched everything unfurl from below. "And one day you'll get everything you deserve!"

"Aw, I don't like to see you so upset, Mildred," he replied, "really I don't. Breaks my heart to see you so distressed, it really does." He paused for a moment, as if in thought. "I'll tell you what I'll do - seeing as I sympathise, and can see you're having a bit of trouble coming to terms with the situation - I'll let you off the hook. You can go - I've got plenty of meat lined up, so losing out on yours won't make a great deal of difference. Naturally, I can't let your little gang of helpers go - my foxy mates would never let me hear the end of it - but I give you my word you can go free, and I'll even let you hang around long enough to say goodbye to them all, before we bung them in the mincer and shoot off round the globe to grab all the other rabbits. I can't say fairer than that, can I?"

He was, of course, toying with the Easter Bunny now. He had destroyed her Easter tradition, her reputation and her business, and was just about to destroy her own kind, by throwing them all into his monstrous mincer. He had seemingly won - utterly - and couldn't be defeated.

"You know as well as I that if my companions go

into your infernal machine, then I shall go with them," she replied, defiantly.

"Fair enough," he shrugged, and gave his foxes the order to throw all the bunnies into the grinder. "You can all be in the first batch of eggs," he grinned. "It'll help us get the flavour right!"

Suddenly, the iron stairwell rocked as a huge explosion shook the main factory. Foxes were flung from the gantry, and many of the helper bunnies managed to wriggle free from their captors. Foxy McFox looked in stupefied anger at the main entrance - its huge doors had been blown off their hinges, leaving an immense cloud of smoke. Then the smoke lifted, revealing a bulky silhouette and many smaller ones to either side.

A voice cried out "Attack!" from the ruptured doorway. It belonged to the Elf Doctor - he was still mounted on Clarence the slug, who reared up like a stallion, before charging forward toward the foxes. They were accompanied by a hundred or more 'ninja' elves - all heavily armoured and even more heavily trained. They carried swords and other martial arts weapons, and were more than ready to take on the evil foxes. Upon the Elf Doctor's command the elves surged forward, shouting "Chaaaaaaarge!"

But Foxy was in no mood to give up all he'd

worked so hard to achieve. "Let's 'ave 'em, lads!" he snarled, as he too ran into battle. With nasty growls and claws at the ready, his foxy mates immediately followed close behind, dropping their captive bunnies so they could leap toward the advancing elves.

And so battle commenced.

CHAPTER NINE

THE ZOMBIE BUNNIES!

The foxes quickly discovered they were in for the fight of their lives. Dealing with rabbits - whether it be the sleepy, docile wild ones or the Easter Bunny's super-smart helpers - had been so easy these past few days, but this strike force of ninja elves was something else entirely. Weaving, bobbing and somersaulting into the air, the nimble elves made it nigh impossible for the clumsier foxes to attack them.

The foxes swiped with razor claws, and gnashed with rows of nasty teeth - but they just couldn't get anywhere near their attackers. The elves meanwhile found the battle most invigorating, and cut and jabbed at the furious foxes with their miniature swords. Foxy's gang yelped and barked as jab after jab pierced their furry hides. Many stealthy elves swung from the rafters on slender ropes, staying out of reach as they continued to inflict punishment on the foxes. A great number of red tails were mercilessly lobbed-off that day, to remind the cruel foxes in days to come of all the wickedness they'd done.

Clarence the slug played his part also, as Santa had predicted he would do. Though he was even more of a mindless eating machine than the wild rabbits, he knew an enemy when he saw one and flattened many a fox with his vast, blubbery body. A great number more lost their footing, thanks to the slippery slime trails he left in his wake. Unable to escape from the slimy gunge in which they'd trodden, these foxes were quickly apprehended by the elves, and tied up so they couldn't cause any more mischief.

The elves didn't get everything their own way, of course - a fair number of Santa's little helpers unfortunately fell in hand-to-claw fighting with the foxes. Indeed, the foxes soon discovered that this was how they fought best - scrappy, vicious close-quarter fighting with the elves was just the sort of thing that foxes were good at.

But the elves began to turn the tide of the battle

in their favour, and soon they weren't alone - for once the Easter Bunny and her helpers had managed to recover from their ordeal atop the mincing machine, they too set about the foxes, just to show them that bunnies should most certainly NOT be treat in such a terrible manner.

Foxy McFox snarled in his rage as he started to realise things were going against him. His foxy mates were having rings run around them by the agile little elves, and were getting trussed up like Christmas turkeys.

"Time for Plan B, then," he growled to himself, and made for the pilot room upstairs.

"He's getting away!" shouted the Elf Doctor, who had been keeping a sharp eye on the ringleader. "After him, elves!"

A small group of elves chased after Foxy, but he was too fast for them as he slunk up the gantry that led upstairs. He slammed the connecting door shut, and locked it from his side.

Once in the pilot room, he immediately set about launching the egg ship from its stationary position in the Gobi Desert. He took off at enormous speed, driving erratically and sending everyone within the vessel spinning and slamming around. Bunnies, foxes, elves and the giant slug were hurled about like rag dolls.

Foxy looked at the digital map in front of the pilot's seat; the nearest place of any note was the Mongolian capital, Ulaanbaatar.

"That'll do nicely," he cackled, and set course. Foxy continued his erratic driving, knowing this would make an assault on the pilot's room almost impossible. And he was right - in the huge factory warehouse on the level beneath him, all was chaos as the various factions continued to be flung from one wall to the next. This continued for what seemed like forever, making everyone feel very queasy indeed.

And then, abruptly, the egg ship ground to a halt. The ship's tannoy pinged and a female, semi-robotic voice announced; "You have reached your destination."

"Eughgh, I feel so sick," groaned the Elf Doctor. So did everyone else, for that matter. "Where ARE we?"

"I haven't a clue," moaned the Easter Bunny weakly, "not without getting into the pilot's room, anyway." Everyone in the factory's production centre feebly sat about, moaning. No-one was in any mood or condition to fight.

After a time, Mildred asked the Elf Doctor how he and the elves had found them.

"We picked up your microwave communication

signal," he explained, "when you contacted the foxes. We'd been scouring the planet, trying to find either yourselves or the egg factory - but your signal helped us quickly zone-in on your whereabouts.

"Of course," answered the Easter Bunny, woozily. "Santa's the only one with a transmitter that matches our own. Thank goodness for that, at least."

Marmaduke spoke next, asking what the course of action was.

"Well, it doesn't look like the foxes have much fight in them now," said the Easter Bunny. She looked over at a heap of groaning foxes - most of them had been tied-up by the elves prior to the egg ship launch. "Let's just bind the last of them, so they don't give us any more bother. But it's Foxy I'm still concerned about."

The Elf Doctor groggily looked up at the stairwell that lead to the pilot's room. "Come on, then," he said weakly, as he and Clarence slowly rose. "Best get this over with."

But as the elf and the Easter Bunny were about to go in search of Foxy, a warning klaxon horn suddenly began to blare. At the same time, smaller warning lights began to flash on the vats full of pink and green chemicals.

"W-what's going on now?" quivered Marmaduke.

"I think it's Plan B," announced Mildred, ominously. "Whatever that is."

Seconds later, the chemical vats were suddenly emptied. The floors beneath the tanks opened up, flushing out all their contents - including the strange-looking bunnies that were floating inside. The rabbits and the fluids all dropped on to the city below, thanks to Foxy pulling a special lever in the cockpit room.

"There's something DIFFERENT about those bunnies," said the Easter Bunny, as she watched them disappear down the holes at the bottom of the fluid tanks. "Foxy's DONE SOMETHING to them - and I don't know what. But I tell you one thing - it's going to be bad for anyone beneath us right now."

And so it turned out. For, as mentioned, the 'anyone' beneath them turned out to be the residents of Ulaanbaatar. They'd looked in wonder at the enormous egg ship hovering above them, and in confusion as thousands of gallons of fluid came raining down on their homes. But soon their looks were ones of horror, as they saw something else rising from the oozing fluids that had fallen from the sky.

More bunnies. Bunnies that could rise from a fall that no-one else could surely get up from. Bunnies that groaned and moaned and staggered but kept coming toward you nonetheless. Bunnies with paws

outstretched and gnashing teeth, and demented eyes that never blinked.

Zombie bunnies.

"Rrrrrrrrrrrrrrr," they moaned, as they lurched forward. "Rrrrrrrrrrrrrrrrrrrrr!"

The people of Ulaanbaatar didn't wait around to investigate these long-eared arrivals. Screaming and shouting, they ran in the opposite direction as the legion of zombie rabbits staggered and hopped, then staggered and hopped some more.

Back on the egg ship, Foxy's snidey voice came over the tannoy. "Just so you know, Mildred, I've just unleashed Plan B. 'What's Plan B?' you may ask. Well, Plan B is what I held back in case things didn't quite work out with my little bunny meat scheme. And, seeing as you, your little elfy friends and that frankly weird slug have caused things to go slightly adrift for me, I saw no alternative but to set Plan B in motion. Now, below us is the rather nice Mongolian capital of Ulaanbaatar - which I've just turned into a zombie-bunny hell hole. Right now, I'm sure they're biting the residents and turning THEM into zombies, too. Give it a week and the whole of Asia will be completely zombiefied, with the rest of the world following shortly after."

Before Foxy could say another word, the door to

the pilot's room was kicked wide open. There stood the Easter Bunny, ready to do battle with her nemesis. As Foxy gloated on the tannoy, she'd crept up the stairwell to confront him, while the Elf Doctor and Clarence were commencing their own mission.

"You really do like the sound of your own voice, don't you?" Mildred growled at Foxy. "Well, it's just you and me now. And mark my words - only one of us will still be standing at the end."

Clarence and the Elf Doctor landed with a heavy squelch in the centre of Ulaanbaatar. They and many of the other elves had activated the emergency parachutes they carried, in order to give chase to the new 'zombie bunnies' that Foxy had seemingly unleashed on the city beneath the egg ship. Some elves had stayed behind on the ship (to assist in keeping the foxes under control), but most were now coming in to land close to where Clarence had touched down.

You may have noticed that Tabitha and Snooks had been a little quiet of late. Well, fear not - for although the rest of the bunnies were still back on the egg ship dealing with the foxes, the 'teenage whingebag' and her geeky companion had decided to tag along with the ninja elves. They'd hitched a ride on the back of Clarence, and were soon lining up

alongside the elves to help take on whatever Foxy had dropped on to the city. And they kept their bickering to a minimum.

The giant slug had landed close to an old missionary church. The Elf Doctor contacted the others on his walkie-talkie, advising them to assemble at the front of the church once they had landed. Within a few minutes, all were gathered together, ready to hunt down the zombie bunnies.

All was deadly quiet, except for an old black crow, who sat cawing on an ancient tree branch. A thick, unseasonal mist clung about them, making the elves shiver. High above their heads, the egg ship hung silent and ominous, and in the distance, several plumes of rising smoke could be seen snaking into the Mongolian sky.

As they were about to depart and begin their hunt, the doors of the church were flung open. The elves turned together to see a wizened old preacher man standing there. The Elf Doctor apologised to him for their intrusion, but the priest told him no apology was necessary.

"I know why you're here, and I know the grave task you have before you," the preacher said, grimly. "I too watch the news - and have seen all that has happened these past few days. And now there walks in this city something far worse than anything that has come before."

The Elf Doctor asked if he had seen any of the zombie bunnies in person. "Look around you, elf," he replied, gesturing to the tombstones that littered the churchyard. They were smeared in the pink and green gunk that had come out of the vats on the egg ship. "Yes, they were here; mere minutes ago - and quickly spread a terror wherever they went. I and my congregation were saved by hiding in the church's catacombs - others were perhaps not so lucky."

The Elf Doctor asked if they needed assistance - but again the preacher indicated otherwise, and told them to hasten on their hunt. "Easter once meant something more than rabbits and chocolates," he sighed, looking up at the cross that hung above his church's doorway. "You must do all you can to stop this menace from spreading - in the hope that the day will come when Easter will once again mean something more."

And so Clarence and the elves set off (with Tabitha and Snooks following close behind). They all mumbled to themselves about what a 'strange oddbod' they thought the old priest had been - but his sombre words stuck in their heads, and their determination to stop the zombie bunnies grew ever stronger.

The zombie trail was not hard to follow. Paw prints and splashes of pink and green goo could be seen from time to time, as could evidence of panic - cars and bicycles lay abandoned, and smoke billowed from buildings where residents had seemingly tried to fight off the zombie bunnies with fire.

In the distance, screams and sounds of panic could be heard. There was an explosion at a gas station - sending a plume of orange fire high into the air, and warning sirens began to wail across the southern outskirts of the city.

The elves quickened their pace, confident they were closing in on the zombie bunnies. They ran along one of the city's main roadways, with panicked people on either side of the street calling out warnings in Mongolian to the advancing elves.

On and on they ran, the street's inhabitants thinning out until eventually no-one could be seen. The road became as silent as the graveyard they had stood in earlier. Then the elves abruptly stopped, as they saw a tiny figure standing in the middle of the road ahead of them.

It spoke. If you could call it speaking ... "Rrrrrrrrrrrrrr."

The small creature moved jerkily, as it slowly turned to face the small unit of elves. It made snarling and moaning noises as it did so, which sent shivers down their spines. It stared at the elves, with sunken, darkened eyes that peered deep into their own. And then it staggered and jumped toward them, gnashing its teeth with every intent of eating its trackers.

It was a zombie bunny. And the first of many, for as soon as its snarling got louder it aroused others that had been foraging in nearby buildings and abandoned vehicles. They came spilling out of cars and buses and homes and businesses and jerked, jumped and shuffled toward Clarence and the line of elves. And they all looked hungry.

"Don't let them bite you," ordered the Elf Doctor, "or you'll get the zombie virus and turn into one of them!"

What followed was pretty horrible indeed. The zombie bunnies had apparently multiplied very quickly since being dropped from the flying egg ship, and were now a seething mass of biting teeth and ragged fur; they looked absolutely terrifying, and the elves needed all their ninja skills to duck and dodge and evade their gnashing teeth and claws. The elves had no guns - only their swords and some martial arts weapons - but using force wasn't the Elf Doctor's plan here.

Before they'd arrived at the egg ship, the elves had equipped themselves with many martial arts weapons.

These included high-powered foam darts (which were not technically martial-arty, but kind of fell into the same category). The darts contained a rapid-dry chemical, which would expand and harden to cement-strength on whatever they made contact with. If you were hit by one, you'd soon be as solid as a statue for a day, until the foam dissolved.

And that's the way the elves dealt with the zombie bunnies. Dart after dart was thrown at the groaning horde of rabbits, solidifying them on the spot. The zombies still moaned and snarled, even after being foamed, but as long as you stayed away from them you stood no chance of getting bitten.

For several hours the elves swept the area, looking for any stray zombies - but eventually the Elf Doctor was able to call in to the North Pole's communications team, and get them to arrange for their removal.

Ulaanbaatar was cleared of the zombie menace, and the foamed-up rabbits were taken out of the city. But then it was a race against time to find an antidote for the virus - after all, the cement foam that held them captive only lasted for a day. An urgent call was put through to the North Pole's science division, to see what they could come up with.

After hours of experimentation, it was discovered the pink and green chemicals that had transformed the bunnies was nothing more than hair gel. Foxy McFox had somehow discovered that rabbits reacted very strangely to the gunk when dropped into a vat of the stuff - it turned them into hideous, zombiefied versions of their original selves. The remedy to cure them was simple; give them a good hose down in cold water, and give them something nice to eat, like a carrot and some lettuce.

"Well, so much for Plan B," Foxy McFox would have said forlornly, had he known how his zombie scheme turned out.

And WHAT OF Foxy McFox, you might ask - and the Easter Bunny, for that matter? Last time we saw them, they were on the verge of their final dual. Well, let's see how all that turned out ...

Hunched-up in the egg ship's pilot seat, Foxy McFox looked very much like the cornered fox he was. Unfortunately, a cornered fox is also a very dangerous one. He'd stolen a sword from one of the elves he had battled with back in the factory, and now lunged forward with all his might at Mildred the Easter Bunny. But all those years of waterskiing had paid off for Mildred, and she managed to twist and turn herself so that the blade just missed her.

"Tut-tut," she said, shaking her head at Foxy,

before revealing a sword of her own (that she always kept deep within the folds of her fur, for extreme emergencies such as this).

And so they fought, sword to sword; they parried and thrusted, jabbed and stabbed, fenced and defended. On and on and on they fought; each one the match of the other, and both showing no sign of weakness. The pilot room was soon a wreck and they moved out to the gantry outside, neither side letting up in the ferocity of their battling.

The tethered foxes and remaining elves and bunnies watched on as the two sworn enemies battled on the stairwell above. No one dared speak lest they cause a fatal distraction.

Far below, the Elf Doctor was beginning his hunt for the zombie bunnies but here, in the egg ship, high up in the clouds, it was a battle to the finish.

But eventually the Easter Bunny began to tire, and she got caught by a nasty cut to the arm. She fell back against the stairwell's supporting rail, and Foxy was quick to move in and finish the job.

"Sorry Mildred," he cackled, "but looks like the little kiddies you love so much are gonna be eating rabbit-flavoured eggs after all." And with that, he lunged his sword at her with all his strength one final time.

But Mildred had been feigning her injury - though cut deep, her wound was not as bad as she had pretended. Once more she twisted and turned as his blade advanced upon her, and Foxy fell headlong over the supporting rail.

Directly beneath was the enormous mincing machine. Its blades were now turning at full pelt, thanks to the hundreds of bunnies turning the giant hamster wheel. As Foxy somersaulted and dropped into the mincer's funnel, his final scream echoed and faded away.

Bunnies and elves rushed to aid Mildred, but she was quite alright really. She was just relieved it was finally all over, as was everyone else.

What came next was the 'mopping-up' - and there was much to do, as billions of bunnies were still running amok. As mentioned earlier, the Elf Doctor had managed to quickly resolve the zombie bunny crisis, and word was sent across the globe that the elves would be dispatching containment tubes to help get the rest of the rabbits under control.

The Easter Bunny received a full pardon from every nation of the world, once word had spread that it had been Foxy McFox who had caused the bunny devastation. It took many weeks, but eventually the billions of extra rabbits were slowly but surely rounded up and moved to a single reservation (deep in the heart of the Gobi Desert, coincidentally enough, which as you may recall had been Foxy's hideout at one point). Mildred ensured they were all well taken care of - she assigned many of her helper bunnies to their upkeep, and they all lived long - and very well-fed - lives. And she stopped fzapping bunnies with her mind-ray - which was very welcome news to all her helpers.

Mildred was of course eternally grateful to Santa and his elves (and Clarence!) - for they had never faltered in their belief she wasn't to blame for all that had happened.

Horatia (the unpleasant lady slug you may remember from the beginning of the book) eventually got rid of her own rabbit invasion, thanks to the elves and their 'bunny collection efforts' (though of course, she was too selfish to ever give them any thanks). The islanders of Oom-Balla-Papa-Lalla-Shaka-Manaloko were soon rid of their bunnies also, along with all the other unfortunates who had suffered during the bunny invasions.

And, despite all that had transpired, Mildred still managed to deliver a PROPER Easter that year - one with scrumptious chocolate eggs for all the children of the world. Though as you can perhaps understand, it had to come a little later than normal - July 17th, to be exact. But of course, no-one really cared about the delay - and once again the Easter Bunny was loved all around the world.

And that's just about all there is to tell about what became known as The Year of the Easter Bunny Invasion.

So if you're reading this story at Easter time, why not call it a day now, and tuck into a delicious chocolate egg instead. But as you're unwrapping that scrumptiously appetising chocolatey treat, I must ask you to spare a thought for Mildred the Easter Bunny and her many friends - for without them, Foxy McFox would have taken over Easter - and you'd be munching on an egg with a very different flavour indeed!

THE END

AUGUSTUS
THE HAIRY
ZUMMABEEST!

THE SLUG
THAT SAVED
CHRISTMAS!

HAIRY
TALES!

THE
EASTER BUNNY'S
UNDERSEA
ADVENTURE!

VERITY
FRUITT AND
MY MAGIC
GONK!

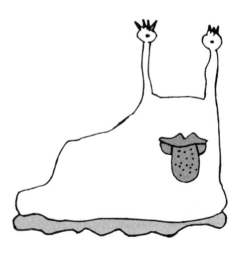

HORRID
HORATIA!

THE
EASTER BUNNY
INVASION!

GRANDMA
GRUNT!

THE
EASTER BUNNY'S
OUTER SPACE
ADVENTURE!

LOOK ON AMAZON
FOR OTHER BOOKS BY
CLIFFORD JAMES HAYES

TSHIRTS AND THOUSANDS OF OTHER PRINTED ITEMS BY CLIFFORD JAMES HAYES

AUDIOBOOKS

Stories full of rhymes, morals and wit - or just plain silliness and absurdity! Great fun for children and adults alike, these crazy tales are brilliantly narrated by New York actor Sheree Wichard.

Available from Amazon.com, Audible and iTunes.

IF YOU LIKED THIS BOOK, PLEASE PUT
A SHORT REVIEW ON THE **AMAZON** WEBSITE
OR THE **CBBC BOOK CLUB**
- THIS WOULD BE **HUGELY APPRECIATED**!

THANK YOU FROM THE AUTHOR

Printed in Great Britain
by Amazon

78410798R00098